'You know, { **simply can** **someone so s** **in St Orvel.'**

Carla smiled a mocking smile. 'Perhaps I missed your civilised and thrilling company.'

'You surprise me. I'd no idea that you found my company civilised.'

He emphasised the last word ever so slightly and pointedly refrained from adding 'and thrilling'. And as a quick, openly provocative flare lit up his eyes Carla suddenly found it extremely hard to hold his gaze.

For she knew what he was remembering. Suddenly, she was remembering it too.

She could hear the thunder crashing, see the lightning cleave the heavens and feel the excitement that raced in her heart. Though it wasn't the wildness of the storm that made her tremble. It was the way he was holding her. The look in his eyes. The impossibly sweet, piercing magic of his kiss.

Stephanie Howard was born and brought up in Dundee in Scotland, and educated at the London School of Economics. For ten years she worked as a journalist in London on a variety of women's magazines, among them *Woman's Own*, and was latterly editor of the now defunct *Honey*. She has spent many years living and working abroad—in Italy, Malaysia, the Philippines and in the Middle East.

Recent titles by the same author:

AMBER AND THE SHEIKH
WAITING FOR MR WONDERFUL!

KISSING CARLA

BY
STEPHANIE HOWARD

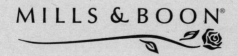

MILLS & BOON®

All the characters in this book have no existence outside the imagination of the author, and have no relation whatsoever to anyone bearing the same name or names. They are not even distantly inspired by any individual known or unknown to the author, and all the incidents are pure invention.

First published in Great Britain 1997
Harlequin Mills & Boon Limited,
Eton House, 18-24 Paradise Road, Richmond, Surrey TW9 1SR

© Stephanie Howard 1997

ISBN 0 263 80617 0

Set in Times Roman 10½ on 11¾ pt.
02-9802-50236 C1

Printed and bound in Great Britain
by Mackays of Chatham PLC, Chatham

CHAPTER ONE

CARLA and Annie were halfway across the car park, heading for Annie's battered old blue Ford, when from the corner of her eye Carla suddenly caught sight of him.

Jedd Hunter. Damn! She felt a dart of dismay. She'd known that at some point she was almost certain to bump into him. St Orvel was little more than a big village, after all. But she'd been hoping she might be lucky. Maybe he'd emigrated to China! And she definitely hadn't expected this stroke of misfortune—that he'd materialise like a bad dream on her very first day!

Still, perhaps she was safe, for it looked as though he hadn't noticed her. A tall, dark-haired figure dressed in jeans and a pale grey T-shirt, he was striding swiftly between the rows of parked cars, making for the dusty Land Rover over in the far corner. Eyes fixed straight ahead, glancing neither left nor right, as though no one in the world existed but him.

So nothing had changed. He was still the same man she'd learned to detest so heartily two years ago. Well, that came as no surprise. Men like Jedd Hunter were set in stone.

But the sight of him was stirring up other emotions as well that were a great deal more unsettling than dislike. A fierce, dark excitement shot with guilt and burning shame was making the blood turn to ice in Carla's veins. For suddenly it was as though she'd been thrown back in time to what, without a single shadow of doubt, was the most ignominious episode of her entire twenty-five years.

So, stop looking at him, she told herself, dropping her gaze away. It was far too nice a day to let it be ruined by the likes of him! The sun was pouring down from a cloudless summer sky, the warm air sharpened by the clean tang of salt that drifted over the town on the gentlest of sea breezes. Only a moment ago, she'd been happily reflecting that her decision to come back here had been the right one, after all. For she had actually wondered about the wisdom of that.

They'd almost reached Annie's car now and Jedd still hadn't spotted her. Carla sighed with relief. She could relax, at least for now. But the very next instant Annie was stopping in her tracks, waving her arms above her head and calling out, 'Jedd! Hi, there! I almost didn't see you!'

As he swivelled round to face them, Carla's heart sank. It had never crossed her mind that her brand-new boss and friend would be acquainted with the odious Jedd Hunter.

Just keep calm, she told herself, and don't let him get to you. She straightened her shoulders, shook back her blonde hair and drew her slim frame up to its full five feet five as he started across the car park towards them. It could have been worse. At least she wasn't on her own. Annie's presence, if nothing else, would oblige him to be civil.

And how he was going to hate that! Inwardly, she

smiled. Hey, maybe this encounter might be quite enjoyable, after all!

'Well, hello there!'

As he greeted Annie, he didn't even glance at Carla, but she knew very well, in spite of that, that he'd recognised her. She could feel his antipathy like a cold hand against her skin.

So, nothing had changed there, either. The feeling was still mutual.

'Carla, let me introduce you.' Annie was turning towards her. 'This is Jedd Hunter. He lives on Pentorra—that lovely island you can see from the harbour. He runs the Pentorra Castle estate. Jedd, this is—'

''I already know who the young lady is.' Before Annie could finish, he quickly cut in and the iron-grey eyes at last fixed on Carla.

Carla felt herself simultaneously freeze and dissolve. She'd entirely forgotten the power of that dark gaze, the way it seemed to sweep you up and carry you away and how pointless it was to try to resist it. She was still desperately trying to catch her breath as he continued, 'My path and Miss Roberts' crossed briefly a couple of summers ago.'

Well, that was one way of putting it! What had actually happened was that Carla had spent two weeks at Pentorra Castle—as the guest of Jedd's cousin Nicholas, a London art dealer, who at that time had been her boyfriend—and by the end of her holiday she and Jedd Hunter had pretty much detested the sight of one another.

Still, you'd never have guessed it as he added with a

false smile, 'What a lovely surprise bumping into you like this.'

Indeed. Carla treated him to a fake smile of her own. 'Precisely what I was thinking,' she replied.

She'd now recovered from the initial impact of looking into his face and, with a sense of cool detachment, was studying him discreetly.

He must be thirty-five now, but he hadn't changed in the past two years. Each harsh line and shadow was just as before. The narrow, deep-set eyes, as hard as river pebbles, the square-hewn jaw, the jutting cheekbones, the wide, harsh mouth. Beneath the sweep of thick, slightly unruly black hair, it was an arresting face, vital and full of character, though far too rough-edged ever to pass as handsome.

That, of course, was an undeniably large part of his appeal. The rawness of his features, the total lack of conventional charm and that dangerous, dark, brooding quality he possessed all somehow combined quite unexpectedly to make him the most alarmingly attractive man Carla had ever set eyes on in her life.

He's quite breathtaking, she thought as she watched him. No wonder I was once seduced—though, naturally, she hastily assured herself, it could never happen again. These days, her dislike of him was far stronger than his allure.

He continued to look at her. 'So, what are you doing in St Orvel? This little corner of Cornwall is surely a bit out of your way?' He paused. 'Perhaps you're just passing through?'

That was obviously what he hoped. Well, she was

about to disappoint him. 'Actually, no. I've got a job here, as a matter of fact.'

'A job?' You could have cracked concrete with the look that crossed his face.

Carla decided to be merciful. 'Only for the summer. I'll be going back to London at the end of August.'

He didn't sigh audibly, but Carla sensed his relief. The tightness around the corners of his mouth relaxed a bit. Damned cheek! If he'd been anyone else, she'd have felt insulted.

'Carla's going to be working with me at the centre.' As Annie offered this information, Carla turned gratefully to look at her, glad of the excuse to detach her gaze from Jedd's. 'She's one of our special summer recruits. She only arrived last night. She's just been helping me run some errands...

'Oh, no!' Interrupting herself, Annie pulled a face. 'I don't believe it! I've left my shopping in the chemist!' She glanced quickly at Carla. 'You wait here and chat to Jedd while I nip back for it. I'll only be a couple of minutes.' Before Carla could utter a word, she was hurrying off.

The atmosphere changed instantly, as though the warm air had been touched with ice.

Carla raised her eyes to his. 'Look, Annie wasn't to know that you and I don't actually have anything to say to each other. So, since I'm sure you've got plenty of other things to do, please don't feel obliged to stick around on my account.'

That was a joke! As though he'd feel obliged to her!

She was the last person he'd be likely to put himself out for!

'I'll tell Annie you had an appointment you had to hurry off to.' She added this just to encourage him on his way.

He remained precisely where he was, not bothering to answer, eyeing her with a look as prickly as barbed wire. Then, finally, he spoke. 'Did I hear correctly? Did Annie just say you're going to be working at the centre?'

It wasn't so much a question as a threat disguised as a challenge. A heavyweight prize-fighter enquiring of some would-be bar-room hero if he seriously intended dropping ash in his beer.

Carla threw him a defiant look. 'That's right. That's what she said. Why? Do you have any objections?'

If he did, her eyes warned him, that was really just too bad. He liked to see himself as the future boss of Pentorra—and to act as though he already was—but, though one day he'd inherit a share of the island, all he was right now was his rich uncle's hired hand, a man with no jurisdiction at all. And, besides, this was St Orvel. Nothing to do with the island. So he could object to her presence as much as he wanted, but he was simply going to have to put up with it.

The steely grey eyes fixed on her. 'You're aware, I presume, that the centre is a summer school for disadvantaged children?' He paused as though he believed this might actually be news to her. 'Of what possible interest could such a place be to you?'

'A great deal, as it happens.' Carla kept her tone even

and let the insult contained in that query wash over her. 'Which is precisely the reason I've taken the job.'

Jedd smiled. That was obviously the best joke he'd heard in ages. 'And you'll be working as a teacher?' This clearly ran a close second.

Carla wished she could hit him. 'Yes,' she said. 'That's the plan.'

He subjected her to another long, penetrating look. 'So, what happened to the PR? Surely, last time we met, you were poised on the brink of a glittering career in that?'

So he hadn't lost his touch. As she remembered all too well, he'd always had a good line in cutting remarks.

But he wasn't worth getting mad at. 'I gave up the PR. I decided I wanted to go back to teaching. I used to be a teacher, you see, before I went into public relations.'

He hadn't known that, of course, but then he knew nothing about her. Not that this somewhat fundamental lack of knowledge had stopped him from making a whole string of damning judgements.

'Did you indeed?' The black eyebrows lifted. Two scornful dark curves above a pair of mocking eyes. 'Now that comes as a surprise. I can't see you as a teacher. Surely PR's much more your sort of thing?

'But no doubt this is only temporary.' Before she could answer, he was carrying on. 'A fill-in measure between jobs or something. You'll be going back to public relations as soon as something comes up?'

'No, I won't.' That short-lived career was behind her. 'I'm back in teaching again for good.'

He seemed to consider this for a moment, clearly far from convinced. 'You mean you plan to give up the glamorous whirl of PR—all the press do's and parties and trips here and there—for the humdrum, low-profile life of a teacher? Clearly, there's a side to your character I somehow missed.'

As he said it, he smiled. He didn't mean a single word. He thought he had her all figured out.

Carla smiled back at him. Let him think what he liked. 'You're wrong. Teaching's really not so humdrum,' she pointed out. 'On the contrary, there are all sorts of unexpected little perks...like getting to come to Cornwall and bump into you, for example.' She fixed him with a look that was sheer unadulterated sarcasm. 'That alone has to be worth giving up all the parties in the world for.'

'I'm flattered you think so.'

His response was to smile—for as Carla had noted many times in the past he could take abuse as well as dish it out. It was a side to his character she reluctantly admired. He was loathsome, but at least he didn't take himself too seriously.

The dark eyes dissected her as he continued. 'But you'll have to forgive me... I still can't quite swallow this sudden, most worthy switch in careers. You see, I happen to know, more or less, what teachers earn, and I really can't see that side of it appealing to you.'

So, he'd got to the point at last. As he continued to watch her, Carla felt a rush of angry resentment. She'd always known what he thought of her, and she hated him for it.

He believed she was the sort of girl who was motivated solely by money. To put it simply and crudely, that she was a nasty little gold-digger.

She breathed slowly for a moment. She wouldn't let him see he'd got to her. His opinion was worth nothing and she'd be crazy to react.

'I suppose you're right about one thing. Compared to my PR days, I've definitely taken a bit of a drop in salary. But I get more than enough reward simply through working with the children.' She added that last bit with a deliberate edge of irony, for she knew he'd never believe her, though it happened to be the truth. The increase in job satisfaction was incalculable.

'I see. So you genuinely are a changed person?' The amused, disbelieving smile remained firmly in place. He narrowed his grey eyes and let his gaze flick over her, taking in her white cotton shirt and lime-green trousers, then coming to settle once more on her face.

Unhurriedly, they travelled over her neat, feminine features. The short, straight nose that was just like her mother's, the generous, soft-lipped mouth that came from her father's side, the wide, long-lashed eyes of a blue that was all her own.

He frowned. 'But there *is* something different about you…' Then he nodded. 'I know what it is… You've cut your hair.'

'I did that some time ago.' Caught momentarily off guard, Carla shook back her ear-length blonde bob a little self-consciously. She'd changed her hairstyle eighteen months ago after ending her relationship with Nicholas. Gone to Michaeljohn in London and got one of their stylists to lop off an uncompromising twenty-five centimetres. A fresh beginning, she'd decided, and a brand-new image to go with it.

'Quite a change. I like it. Much more stylish.' He paused, seemed to consider for a moment, then shook his head. 'You know, for the life of me, I simply can't imagine what someone so stylish is doing here in St Orvel. Surely the big city's the natural habitat of a girl like you? What on earth prompted you to abandon the bright lights of London?'

'Like I said, maybe I was hoping to bump into you.' Carla smiled a mocking smile. 'As you must be aware, I always found our encounters so terribly uplifting. Perhaps I missed your civilised and thrilling company.'

'You surprise me. I'd no idea that you found my company civilised.'

He emphasised the last word ever so slightly and pointedly refrained from adding 'and thrilling'. And as a quick, openly provocative flare lit up his eyes Carla suddenly found it extremely hard to hold his gaze. You fool, she chastised herself. You handed him that one on a plate.

For she knew what he was remembering. Suddenly, she was remembering it too.

The two of them on the boat, the storm lashing, the sky as black as night. She could hear the thunder crashing, see the lightning cleave the heavens and feel the excitement that raced in her heart. Though it wasn't the wildness of the storm that made her tremble. It was the way he was holding her. The look in his eyes. The impossibly sweet, piercing magic of his kiss.

Horror seized her at the memory. It had been a moment of sheer lunacy and he was totally wrong to make the assumption he was making. Hell would freeze over before there was any chance at all of anything similar ever happening again. And, since the subject had been dragged up, it might be wise to set him straight.

She tilted her chin at him. 'Of course, you're absolutely right. Civilised is not a word I'd use to describe you. To tell the truth, the *only* way I'd ever describe you…' she paused to make certain he'd picked up that 'only' '…is as someone I'd prefer to have nothing at all to do with.'

Before he could cut in, she snatched a quick breath. 'And, to return to what we were talking about, I ought to point out that I really don't have to answer to you for my movements. My reasons for being here are no concern of yours.'

Abruptly, his expression hardened. 'I'd like to think you were right. Believe me, I have no wish to get involved in your affair. So, just answer me one thing…' He fixed her with a probing look, the dark eyes virtually narrowed to pinpoints. 'You're not planning, by any chance, to visit Pentorra while you're here?'

The honest answer to that was no. The island of Pentorra was owned by Nicholas's and Jedd's uncle Jasper, a feisty old man who lived in the huge castle there and with whom Carla had struck up a warm friendship during her holiday. He'd told her at least a hundred times that she'd be welcome back any time. But, as much as she'd have loved to take up his invitation, for it would have meant a lot to her to see him again, Carla had come to the conclusion that it would be better to stay away.

What if Nicholas was there? That would definitely be a bit tacky. Things hadn't exactly ended amicably between them.

So she could have satisfied Jedd easily, simply by telling him the truth. But satisfying Jedd wasn't on her agenda.

She threw him a rebellious look. 'I hadn't actually thought about it. But, now that you mention it, it might be rather a nice idea.'

'Think again.' His tone had grown as harsh as sandpaper. He seemed to take a threatening step towards her. 'I'm afraid you wouldn't be welcome on Pentorra.'

'By whom? By you? That's sure to give me sleepless nights!' He hadn't actually moved. He was just leaning closer. But if he was trying to intimidate her he wouldn't succeed. 'Your feelings on the matter don't concern me, I'm afraid. Only Jasper's feelings count and I know he'd be glad to see me.''

'You think so, do you?'

'I'm absolutely sure of it.'

'Yes, I seem to remember you made quite a hit with the old man.'

He paused as a dark look fell across his eyes. The shadow of some black thought she could sense churning round his brain. Then he demanded, 'Have you come here looking for Nicholas, by any chance?'

'Absolutely not!' Where had he got that idea from? 'Things have been over between Nicholas and me for a long time.'

'You've had a pointless journey if you have. He's not here and he won't be coming. He's on the other side of the world—in South America—at the moment. So if you came with a view to rekindling your romance you may as well forget it and just go straight back home.'

Was he deaf or something? Carla sighed with impatience. 'I assure you that nothing could be further from my mind. The only reason I'm here is to work at the centre, and if I was to go to the island it wouldn't be to look for Nicholas. It would just be because I'd like to see Jasper.'

'Would you, indeed?' Jedd remained silent for a moment. Then, frowning thoughtfully, he nodded his head. 'Yes, I think I'm beginning to get the picture.'

'What picture?'

'Why you're here.'

'Well, congratulations! I've told you twice!'

'Yes, you have. But, for some reason, your version fails to convince me. I think, on reflection, that I much prefer my own.'

'Which is?' As she looked at him she felt her heart falter. The steely eyes were filled with undisguised contempt. 'No, on second thoughts, don't bother to tell me,' she amended. 'I can live without knowing what nasty little theory you've come up with.' Was she a masochist or something to actually *invite* his insults?

He'd clearly had no intention of elaborating anyway. 'All you need to know is this. Don't come to Pentorra. And, above all, don't try to come anywhere near the old man.'

Carla glared at him. 'Oh really? And what'll happen if I do?'

'You'll have me to deal with. That's what'll happen.' This time, he did take a step towards her. 'So I'd advise you to listen very carefully to what I've just told you.'

He was standing so close she could feel the heat of him press against her. The scent of him filled her nostrils, making it difficult to breathe.

'You see, you've wasted your time coming here.' His voice was low and menacing. 'Your clever little plan is destined to come to nothing.'

What plan? What was he talking about? Did he still believe she'd come to find Nicholas? But, before she could ask, he was turning away, delivering one final parting shot over his shoulder as he went.

'The best thing you could do is go back to London. I'm sure Annie would have no trouble finding a replacement and your departure would save us all a great deal of unpleasantness.'

He paused. 'Believe me, I'd take it very seriously if you were to do anything so rash as ignore what I've just said.' Then, with a final black look, he strode off towards his car.

Carla watched him, still catching her breath, as he reached it and climbed inside. And her heart rate didn't actually return to normal until a good couple of minutes after he'd driven away.

Jedd, too, was having trouble with his heart rate. His knuckles were white as they angrily gripped the steering wheel and it was an effort to keep his foot from slamming down hard on the accelerator.

Damned woman! Why in heaven's name did she have to turn up now? He had other things on his mind than having to keep an eye on her. But he had no choice now. It was essential that he keep her away from Pentorra.

He headed down to the seafront, near the old harbourmaster's building, and pulled in at the roadside while he tried to collect his thoughts. This was one of his favourite spots. The view was spectacular. Even in winter, except when it was foggy, you could see right across the bay to the island. He often came here just to drink in the beauty of it.

Right now, though, he didn't give the view a second glance. He stared blindly through the windscreen, brows knitted together. He regretted the way he'd let fly at her like that. It had been a bit over the top. There'd been no need to come the heavy. And, besides, it had been entirely the wrong line of approach. She had much too much spirit to cave in under threats.

He smiled to himself. It had been quite a shock when he'd caught sight of her standing there in the car park beside Annie. She was the last person he'd ever expected to see back in St Orvel—though, to be honest, his instant reaction hadn't been entirely negative. In fact, if only circumstances had been a little different, her stay might have provided an intriguing diversion. But the way things were she was simply a headache he could happily do without.

He sighed and turned at last to gaze out to sea, his mood instantly easing at the sight of Pentorra off in the distance. Pentorra. The thing he loved most in all the world.

It was a pity she was going to be working at the centre—a revelation that still struck him as exceedingly bizarre—for the link with Annie would definitely complicate things a bit. He frowned. He'd have to be extra careful from now on.

As for the rest? Well, he'd been perfectly serious in what he'd said. If Carla went ahead and tried any of her little tricks, he'd see to it that she was instantly stopped.

Once more calm, his earlier fury replaced by cool resolve, he slipped the Land Rover into gear and set off down the road again.

CHAPTER TWO

AFTER Jedd had stormed off and she'd recovered her composure, Carla made herself a solemn promise. From now on, as far as she was concerned, Jedd Hunter did not exist.

If she ever had the misfortune to bump into him again—if she even as much as spied him off in the distance—she'd dive up a side-street or cross the road to avoid him. She never wanted to look into his odious face again!

And he really needn't worry about keeping her off his precious island, though he was kidding himself if he thought for one minute that he could scare her. If she wanted to go, she'd go. She didn't give a damn about his stupid threats!

But what had all that been about anyway? All those strange accusations. That she had some secret reason for coming here. Some clever little plan. It was just too bizarre. It made no sense at all.

She pushed it from her mind. I refuse even to think about it, she told herself. What normal, sane person could even begin to guess at what went on inside Jedd Hunter's impossibly warped brain? Besides, she was forgetting—he didn't exist!

Unfortunately, a couple of minutes later, when Annie

got back to the car park, the first thing she asked was, 'Where's Jedd gone? Why didn't he wait?'

Carla swallowed a grimace. 'He had to rush off. Maybe he had an appointment or something.'

A harmless lie, she decided, privately reflecting that Annie had actually sounded quite disappointed. Don't say the poor girl was one of his misguided admirers? But, though she was suddenly rather curious, she didn't enquire. Instead, she hurriedly changed the subject.

'Oh, good, I see you got your shopping back okay.'

But, alas, that wasn't the end of it. As they drove back to the centre, Annie turned to her and demanded, 'How come you know Jedd?'

Oh, dear. Like a dose of flu, he wasn't so easy to shake off.

Carla took a deep breath. 'We met that time I was here on holiday.' She'd already told Annie, back at the interview, that she'd visited the area a couple of years ago. 'But I couldn't actually say I *know* him,' she added quickly, hoping this might discourage any further questions. 'I mean, we're not friends or anything like that.'

How about that for a nice bit of understatement?

'So you didn't visit the island? What a pity. You missed out. But if you like I'll ask Jedd if you can go over while you're here. I know you'd love it. It's just so beautiful.'

'Oh, don't bother. Really.' Wouldn't that just be a treat! 'I'm sure I'm going to be far too busy for that.'

'Nonsense! Of course you're not. What do you think I am—a slave-driver?' Annie laughed and flicked her an amused, chastising look. 'I'll definitely speak to Jedd. In fact, I'll give him a ring tonight.'

'Really, no. I'd rather you didn't—' Carla broke off with a small sigh. This was starting to get silly. It was time to come clean. At least, about the essentials.

'Actually, I have been to the island.' She pulled a contrite face. She hadn't been intending to keep it a secret—even less to deliberately mislead Annie—but the subject simply hadn't come up before. 'That time I came on holiday... I was a guest at the castle.'

Annie laughed, her eyebrows lifting. 'Well, you're a dark horse! A guest at the castle, no less! So, you know the old man?'

'Yes, I do, though I didn't before I went to stay with him. You see, at that time, I was friendly with his nephew Nicholas.'

'Ah. So you know Nicholas.' For the first time ever, Carla was aware of a cool note in Annie's voice. Then, almost as though she'd been aware of it herself, she added quickly, her expression warm again, 'So, you're familiar with the island. Isn't it an amazing place?'

Carla smiled. 'Just about the most amazing place I've ever seen.'

That was the truth. She still vividly remembered sitting on the boat on the journey across, watching the island get closer and closer and being totally bowled over by its sheer magical beauty. The whitewashed, red-tiled houses sparkling in the sun, the rolling, lush green hills rising up behind and, of course, the splendid castle, perched high on a rocky promontory, guarding the narrow strait as it had for three hundred years. She'd fallen in love with it right there and then.

It was a love affair that had intensified with every single day of a holiday she would always remember and treasure. The only fly in the ointment had been Jedd.

She was just thinking this when Annie suddenly turned to her and said, 'Isn't it sad about Jasper? I hear they're saying there's not much hope.''

'What do you mean?' Carla swivelled round with a start to face her. 'What's wrong with him? Is he ill? I'd no idea.'

'Didn't you? Oh, dear. He's been poorly for a while now. He caught a chest infection and at his age…'

Carla was a little surprised at how deeply shocked she felt. After all, it was two years since she'd seen the old man. But she'd liked him enormously, had felt a real, genuine closeness, and, to be perfectly honest, when she and Nicholas had broken up, one of the things that had saddened her most had been knowing she'd probably never see Jasper again.

For the rest of the day she felt quite haunted by Annie's news. It was terrible. Poor Jasper. She had to go and visit him.

But what about Jedd and his warning to stay away? The last thing she wanted was to provoke some ugly scene that might inadvertently involve the old man. That would be unforgivable. She simply couldn't risk it. So, perhaps it might be wiser if she kept away, after all, and sent him a note and a bunch of flowers instead? Yet that didn't seem enough. It was too impersonal, somehow.

Carla was still worrying about what to do when she

finally went to bed. But as she lay there, her brain churning, something else clicked into place.

Jedd had told her to stay away from the island and the old man. He'd said she'd wasted her time coming, that her plans would come to nothing. At the time, she'd been totally baffled. But not any more.

It was so obvious, really. He'd always considered her a gold-digger. And now, though it made her flesh crawl to think it, it was plain that he believed she'd come to St Orvel in order to try and profit from the old man's imminent death.

As the enormity of it sank in, Carla lay rigid beneath the bedclothes. How could anyone, even Jedd, suspect such a vile thing?

Jedd's bad opinion of her dawned on Carla only gradually during the course of that holiday two years ago.

To begin with, he was perfectly polite, if a little distant—which Nicholas told her was just the way he was with everyone. And it was true. Though there was an element of directness in his manner, a simple straightforwardness that she actually rather liked, she was aware at the same time of a strong sense of separateness in him. He was friendly enough with Nicholas and Nicholas's older sister, Henrietta, for example, but he never spent a great deal of time with them.

'I don't think he really approves of his London cousins,' Nicholas explained light-heartedly. Henrietta, like himself, was based in the capital, though she invariably spent the summer months on Pentorra. 'He seems to think we get up to all sorts of disgraceful things.'

So, at first, Carla thought nothing of Jedd's faint cool-ness towards her—perhaps he disapproved of her too, just because she was Nicholas's girlfriend! But then she started picking up little hints here and there that made her come to realise there was a lot more to it than that.

One evening, when they were all having dinner to-gether, Jasper suddenly asked Nicholas about his new flat in Sloane Square.

'It's fabulous,' Nicholas told him. 'Much more room than my old place.' He turned with a smile to glance at Carla. 'And it's so handy for all our favourite shops and restaurants.'

Out of politeness, Carla simply nodded in agreement. The truth was it was handy for all *Nicholas's* favourite shops and restaurants! Not that she didn't like them. They were just slightly beyond her pocket! But as Nicholas went on to tell his uncle more about his new flat Carla was suddenly aware of Jedd's eyes watching her from across the table.

As she half turned to face him, his gaze flicked over her, as though he was assessing her linen blouse and matching skirt. Carla suspected that, unlike the people Nicholas hung out with who could spot a Chanel or Gucci label in the dark at fifty paces, Jedd was probably unaware that her outfit sported the latter, but he'd know it wasn't the sort of thing a PR assistant could easily afford. And it appeared from his expression that he was putting two and two together and coming up with the conclusion that Nicholas had bought it for her, from one of those favourite shops he'd just mentioned.

She felt herself flush with annoyance. Nothing could

be further from the truth. She'd never allowed Nicholas to buy her fancy presents or to shower her with expensive designer clothes. Her outfit had been a find at a second-hand thrift shop, just like the Jill Sander dress she'd been wearing last night, and had set her back a mere fraction of its original price—for she'd paid for it with her own money, not with Nicholas's gold card. She wished she could say something, but it was scarcely the time or place—and, anyway, why should she feel the need to explain herself to Jedd?

There was another little incident a couple of days later when Nicholas was talking about how he'd booked a box at the Royal Opera House for the first night of a new production of *Rigoletto*. 'Nothing but the best is good enough for Carla,' he said, casting a quick, teasing wink in her direction.

Well, I don't know about that. I'd be just as happy in the gods. Carla opened her mouth to say it, but she never got the chance. For suddenly Jasper was asking her, 'So you're an opera fan, are you?'

'Oh, yes. I love it.' With a smile, she turned to answer him, but not before she'd caught the mocking look on Jedd's face. *Nonsense*, it seemed to say. *What she really loves is going to first nights and sitting in the best seats!*

Ignoring him, she added, 'It's a real passion of mine.'

It was an enthusiasm she'd picked up from her adored Italian mother who, throughout Carla's childhood, had filled their little council house with the magical strains of Verdi and Puccini. Carla had known all the words from the famous arias of *Rigoletto* long before she'd managed to master 'Three Blind Mice'!

She was about to tell Jasper this, but as a sudden black grief descended on her she no longer trusted herself to speak. Just over six months ago, her whole world had crumbled when, after a long, cruel illness, her mother had died.

So, once again, she'd failed to put Jedd right. Though, perversely, the more she began to suspect his opinion of her, the less inclined she actually felt to defend herself. His opinion didn't matter to her. Let him think what he liked!

It was one afternoon at the end of her first week, as she was sitting out on the terrace reading a book— Nicholas was off visiting an out-of-town client—that Jedd appeared unexpectedly and asked, 'Do you mind if I join you?'

'Of course not.' Carefully hiding her surprise, Carla closed her book as he seated himself opposite her. What on earth was this all about?

It started off civilly enough. He leaned forward in his cane chair. 'So, are you enjoying your stay on Pentorra?' he asked.

'Very much.' She smiled at him. 'It's a wonderful place.'

'Yes, it is.' He smiled back—that rare, powerful smile that had taken her by surprise the first time she'd seen it. In spite of all his faults, she'd found herself thinking, I'll bet there's no shortage of women falling at his feet.

'So,' he continued, 'you don't mind being left on your own?'

'Not at all. I quite enjoy a bit of my own company.

And I knew Nicholas was going to be busy a lot of the time, so I brought along a supply of books.'

'Very wise.' He nodded towards the book in her lap. 'So, what's that one you're reading at the moment?'

'Just a light-hearted romance. A bit of escapism.' Carla told him the name of the author and the title. 'It's very good, though I don't suppose it's your sort of thing.'

Jedd shook his head. 'No, I don't suppose it is. What is it? One of those tales about how the poor heroine catches her man?'

Instantly, an alarm bell went off in her brain. She kept her gaze steady. 'Actually no,' she told him. 'It's really more about how the poor hero catches the girl.'

'I see. A twist on the more conventional plot.'

This novelty appeared to amuse him for a moment. He leaned back, long legs stretched out in front of him, tilting his head as he studied her face. Then he asked, 'How did you come to meet my cousin?'

It sounded like a perfectly innocent question, but something was telling her it was nothing of the sort. How did a working-class girl from the East End of London manage to catch herself a wealthy heir like my cousin? That was what he was really asking! For, one day, Nicholas, jointly with Jedd, would inherit the valuable Pentorra estate.

Was it a class thing? she suddenly wondered. Was he so willing to think badly of her because she came, as it were, from the wrong side of the tracks? That would have surprised her. He definitely wasn't her favourite person, but he'd never, even remotely, struck her as being a snob.

'I met him at a party,' she explained, answering his question. 'Through some mutual friends from work.' She fought the temptation to go on and point out that at the time she'd known nothing at all about Nicholas's background and that it was he who, with great determination, had pursued her. There really was no way she was going to stoop to defending herself!

Besides, she'd already decided it probably wouldn't make any difference. He'd still continue to look down his arrogant nose at her. Nicholas had told her he frowned on people who enjoyed their kind of lifestyle.

'Just because he goes around in jeans and T-shirts all the time and thinks a grand social occasion's a walk in the woods with his dog, he seems to believe that everybody else should be equally unassuming in their tastes,' he'd declared.

Carla had smiled at this piece of blatant exaggeration. Jedd definitely leaned towards the casual end of the sartorial spectrum and he was obviously very fond of Buster, his black Labrador, who followed him around like a faithful shadow most of the time, but she suspected he wasn't quite as easy to pigeon-hole as that. Still, she could appreciate what Nicholas was talking about.

She'd noticed how Jedd would sometimes look disapprovingly at his cousin when he mentioned some top-class restaurant he'd recently been to or referred to an exotic holiday abroad. Even she often found Nicholas's habits a bit extravagant, but surely it was his right to spend his own money as he chose? It definitely wasn't any business of Jedd's.

He was continuing to watch her, 'So, tell me,' he enquired, 'how are you enjoying life in Sloane Square? That new flat of Nicholas's certainly sounds pretty grand.'

'It is. It's magnificent.' Carla straightened in her seat. This time, she definitely would put him right. 'However, you're wrong about one thing. I'm afraid I don't live there. It just so happens I have my own flat—a rather more modest affair in Arnos Grove.'

He looked surprised for a moment, but then he said with a shrug, 'Oh, well, no doubt it's only a matter of time. As Nicholas was saying just the other day, Sloane Square's so handy for all your favourite shops and restaurants.'

It was just at that moment, before Carla could protest that she'd no intention of ever moving into Nicholas's flat, that Mrs Pickles, the housekeeper, appeared on the terrace to tell Jedd he was wanted on the phone.

He stood up at once, as though grateful to remove himself from Carla's company. 'I'll take it indoors,' he told Mrs Pickles. Then he cast Carla a quick glance. 'I'll let you get back to your book.' And, with that, he walked off, leaving her fuming in silence.

After that conversation, Carla was convinced. His dislike of her wasn't just because he disapproved of her lifestyle or because she happened to be Nicholas's girl-friend. And it had nothing whatsoever to do with class either. No, it was purely personal. That was very plain indeed. For some reason, he'd decided she was a nasty little gold-digger.

For most of the night, Carla lay awake recalling these events, angry with Jedd and furious at herself.

She shouldn't have been so proud. She ought to have defended herself, made it clear that he was wrong, that she wasn't that sort of girl, then maybe now he wouldn't be thinking all these awful things about how she'd come to St Orvel to try and fleece the old man. Each time she remembered that, she felt physically ill.

The next morning, however, she tried to put it from her head. She had other things to think about and it would do her no good anyway. On the contrary, if she continued, she'd drive herself mad.

So as she sat on her wooden bench at the edge of the playground, which positively vibrated with excited voices and running feet, she wasn't thinking of Jedd or any of the stuff he'd said. She was simply reflecting on how good it felt to be here.

Today was her first day of actually working with the children and already she was loving every single exhausting minute. She'd never felt so enthusiastic about any job before.

It was funny, but she'd known from the start it would be like this—right from the moment when her friend Sally in London had told her about the ad she'd seen in the local press.

A privately run centre in Cornwall for disadvantaged children had been looking for temporary summer staff. As a geography teacher in one of the poorer areas of the capital, Carla was already involved with such children and their problems. This is for me, she'd thought instantly. Her search for a summer job was over.

She'd had only one very brief moment of hesitation and that was when she'd discovered that the Starship Centre, which had only been open since Easter last year, was actually situated on the outskirts of St Orvel. It might be a bit embarrassing if she were to bump into Nicholas and it would definitely be most unpleasant to bump into Jedd.

But she'd quickly dismissed these qualms. She'd be spending most of her time at the centre and, even if she did meet either or both of them, she was surely quite capable of handling the encounter?

So she'd sent off her application, gone along to the interview and, to her immense delight, received a letter a week later telling her that she was one of the lucky six to be chosen. And now here she was, sitting out in the July sunshine, helping to supervise the children's post-lunchtime break after one of the most satisfying mornings she'd ever known.

She let her gaze drift over the noisy playground where the entire sixty children who'd be here throughout the summer—thirty boys and thirty girls, all between the ages of seven and twelve—were playing in groups with their skipping ropes and balls. Most of them had arrived yesterday or, like herself, the day before, and right now she still had trouble remembering some of their names. But she was looking forward to getting to know all of them over the coming five weeks.

Something else she was looking forward to was working with her six colleagues, especially Annie, her freckle-faced boss. From the moment she'd met her—at the interview in London—she'd taken a huge liking to the dedicated twenty-nine-year-old. She ran the place with the help of a young secretary and a couple of cooks and, right now, she was at the other end of the playground overseeing a group of girls.

Carla glanced across at her—and instantly found herself remembering what Annie had told her yesterday about Jasper. That provoked a dart of guilt, for she still hadn't decided whether or not she ought to go and visit him. Damn Jedd! It would all be so straightforward if it wasn't for him!

At that moment, her attention was caught by the sound of raised voices. Red-haired Freddie, who she'd noticed seemed to have difficulty making friends, appeared to be involved in a heated discussion about a ball. He and another ten-year-old were standing glaring at one another. Any minute now, blows were about to be exchanged.

She got up and headed towards them. 'What's the matter?' she called out. Let's see if she could work a bit of peace-making magic!

Easier said than done. A couple of minutes later, she was still trying to pacify two angry little boys. Then the bell rang for the next class and she heaved a sigh of relief.

'We'll sort this out properly later,' she told them as everyone lined up to go back inside. 'Come on, let's just forget about it for now.'

She watched them as they headed off, still scowling,

but at least not hitting each other, and was aware of a warm, satisfied glow deep inside her. Working here was going to be a challenge. Some of these children were far from easy. But it promised to be by far the most rewarding job she'd ever done.

Smiling, she reached inside her bag for her timetable, just to double-check which room she ought to be going to. And, in that instant, she realised that she'd come to a decision.

Hang Jedd's stupid veto! He'd no right whatsoever to try and stop her going to the island! She hadn't been planning to go, but now she had a duty to. An old man who, two years ago, had welcomed her into his home and treated her with enormous generosity and kindness was lying ill, less than half an hour's boat ride away. It would be an absolute disgrace if she didn't go and see him.

She stuffed her timetable back in her bag and strode up the steps. She'd go tomorrow, after lunch. She had a couple of hours free then.

'Hop in, miss. There's room for two more.'

Carla took the strong, rough hand that was held out to her and stepped down into the gently swaying ferry. 'Thanks,' she told the pilot, and went to seat herself in the stern next to a smiling woman with a bulging shopping bag—probably an employee or the wife of one of the employees on the estate.

For this was the little ferry that, five times a day, made its way back and forth between St Orvel and the island, carrying the residents and their visitors and the mobile library and the postman and whoever else needed to get from one side to the other—though it could only take a maximum of four cars on each trip! Carla had remembered about the ferry from last time she was here, though this was the first time she'd actually been on it. She and Nicholas had always used one of Jasper's private launches.

The pilot was glancing at his watch, then up at the tiny quay. There was still one seat free and he tended to wait till the boat was full. In these parts, no one was too worried about leaving dead on time.

Carla followed his gaze, clutching the bag of fruit she'd bought for Jasper, aware of a tiny flutter of nerves. She was doing the right thing—she was convinced of that now—but, when she got to the island, please don't let her bump into Jedd!

At that instant, her heart stopped.

With a gasp of horror, she blinked.

Surely she must be seeing things? This couldn't be true.

But it was. Holding her breath, feeling her face turn paper-pale, Carla gaped in dismay at the tall, dark-haired figure who was striding along the quayside, heading for the boat. Jedd. She felt like turning and diving overboard.

Breathing carefully, she lowered her gaze, eyes fixed blindly on the wooden deck, the sound of his approaching footsteps exploding like gunshot in her ears. It was a disaster. Her mission was over before it had begun. For, as soon as he spotted her—and he would the instant he stepped aboard—he'd insist that she disembark, if he didn't actually throw her off himself! Nothing in the world was surer than that.

There was a movement. Any second, she'd feel his hand on her arm, hear the angry bark of his voice in her face. Anxiously, she waited, her heart clattering against her ribs.

But nothing at all happened. Instead, she was aware of a slight vibration and the gentle purr of the ferry's engine.

She glanced up. They were casting off, rapidly heading out to sea. And Jedd, who'd obviously never intended coming aboard, was now almost at the end of the quay.

She slumped back in her seat, grinning like an idiot. She was safe! There would be no confrontation with Jedd after all!

Carla stepped from the ferry and gazed around her in sheer delight. It was all just as perfect and magical as she remembered. The sights, the smells, the very taste of the place! It felt absolutely wonderful to be back.

It was a good fifteen-minute walk to the castle—past the terrace of whitewashed houses that lined the narrow quayside, then up a steep winding road shaded by tall sycamores, till you finally came to the tall wrought-iron gates. There were few taxis and no buses at all on Pentorra—just about everyone had their own car—so, unless you could manage to organise a lift, the easiest way to get around was on foot!

Carla set off at a quick stride, actually quite relishing the walk. It was all part of life here and she loved everything about it. Besides, she'd remembered to wear sensible flat shoes!

She was about halfway up the winding road when a woman's voice called out her name.

In surprise, Carla spun round—there was something familiar about that voice—and saw that a low open sports car had stopped alongside her.

'I thought it was you!' came the friendly greeting from the driver's seat. 'How lovely to see you! What are you doing on Pentorra?'

'Henrietta!' Delighted, Carla hurried over to greet her. 'It's great to see you, too! And you're looking wonderful as usual.' She'd always thought Nicholas's elegant chestnut-haired sister would look good in a bin bag!

'Jump in!' Henrietta was pushing open the passenger door. 'I was down at the quay to pick up a parcel from the boat and I caught a glimpse of you but thought I must have made a mistake.' As Carla climbed in and slammed the door shut, she continued with a laugh, 'But just now, driving up behind you, I could see it was you, after all—even though you've gone and cut off all your hair.' She flashed her a smile. 'I like it. It's very chic.'

'Thanks.' As Carla smiled back at her, it flickered through her mind that Jedd had said more or less the very same thing. But she pushed the thought away. Thinking of Jedd Hunter gave her a headache. And she'd no reason to think of him. He was over in St Orvel, never suspecting for one moment that she was defying his taboo!

'I heard about Jasper,' she told Henrietta, answering

her earlier query. 'I just had to come over and see how he was.'

As they headed up the road, she went on to explain that she'd come to Cornwall to work at the Starship Centre for a few weeks and that it was Annie who'd told her about the old man.

'I was absolutely stunned. Is he really as bad as they say?'

'He's pretty bad, I'm afraid.' Henrietta cast her a sober glance. 'But I, for one, haven't given up hope yet. He's over the worst of the infection and he has the occasional good day. Of course, he's terribly weak—the infection really took it out of him—but he's a fighter, as I'm sure you know.' As she paused, her expression relaxed just a little. 'He's going to be so pleased to see you.'

Henrietta parked the car in the gravel forecourt in front of the castle, which was every bit as grand and imposing as Carla remembered with its tall stone turrets and ivy-clad walls.

'I'll take you up to see him.' She took Carla by the arm and began to lead her up the steps. 'We probably oughtn't to stay long. As you'll appreciate, he tires easily. But, before you leave, maybe we can fit in a quick cup of coffee and a chat?'

'I'd like that.' Carla smiled back at her as they headed into the main hall, all heavy wood panelling and wrought-iron sconces. She was even more glad than ever now that she'd decided to come, for it would be nice to renew her friendship with Henrietta, who, during her stay here, couldn't have been nicer to her.

They headed up the double curved mahogany staircase, then turned into a narrow corridor lit by a tall casement window. Slanting rays of sunshine dappled the silk-clad walls.

At last, Henrietta stopped outside a door near the end. 'We're here.' She frowned at Carla and laid a hand on her arm. 'Now prepare yourself. He's no longer the same man you knew two years ago.'

Carla nodded. 'Don't worry.' Then she took a deep breath as Henrietta pushed open the door and invited her to go in first.

A moment later, she froze, nearly dropping her bag of fruit. She'd been prepared for a shock, but she hadn't expected this.

Horror poured through her. She just stood there and stared, though she hadn't even glanced yet at the frail figure in the bed. For she couldn't take her eyes off the man in the high-backed chair who, for a moment, had looked every bit as astonished as she was, though his surprise had turned instantly to raw, smouldering fury.

She felt her stomach turn to cinders. This was a disaster. It was Jedd.

CHAPTER THREE

CARLA was wishing she could just melt into the green Chinese carpet. He must have come over on one of the private launches. What an idiot she was. She hadn't thought of that.

'I'll see you later.' Behind her, Henrietta whispered apologetically. Next instant, the door clicked shut and she was gone.

Oh, dear. Why on earth had Henrietta disappeared? Now she didn't even have an ally to support her!

'I thought I warned you.' Jedd's eyes drove into her. 'What the hell are you doing here?'

'I've come to see Jasper.' Carla straightened as she spoke and was pleasantly surprised at the calmness of her own voice. 'Not that it's any of your business,' she added sharply, for she was growing a little tired of forever being required to justify her presence to Jedd Hunter!

There was a silence. Carla could hear her heart beating like a hammer. I know what he's about to do, she thought. It was written all over his face and in the muscularly poised, threatening way he was sitting. He's going to get up out of that chair, grab me by the scruff of the neck and throw me bodily back out into the corridor. And, sadly, there isn't a single thing I can do to stop him.

For how could she make a fuss or even think about

fighting him—which was what every single fibre of her body ached to do—with Jasper, lying just a few feet away in his sickbed?

Resigned, she tensed inwardly and waited for the assault.

But then, quite suddenly, the old man spoke.

'Who's that?' He craned forward from the pile of pillows that propped him up. 'Someone's there. Who is it? I can hear them,' he insisted. His voice was as thin and weak as a baby bird's.

It's no one and she's just leaving. Before Jedd had time to say it—for Carla could sense the words forming in his head—she took a deep breath and butted in quickly.

'It's me. Carla Roberts. I've come to see how you are.'

'Who? Who did you say it was?' Jasper peered in her direction. 'I can't see you, whoever you are. Come a little closer, if you don't mind.'

As Carla stepped forward, suddenly Jedd moved. She felt a quick dart of alarm. Was he about to pounce on her, after all? But no, he was simply turning to the bedside table at his elbow. As he leaned over it, he seemed to be searching for something.

'It's Carla Roberts,' she heard him say. 'Nicholas's old girlfriend. Remember, she came to stay with us a couple of summers ago?'

'Carla who?'

The old man was still obviously none the wiser. He continued to stare with a blank look at where she was standing. Inwardly, Carla squirmed. Help, he didn't even remember her! Maybe she shouldn't have come, after all. But at that moment Jedd suddenly found what he'd been looking for—a pair of small, wire-framed spectacles—and leaned forward to prop them, ever so gently, on the old man's nose.

'Carla Roberts,' he said again. 'Nicholas's friend. From London.'

But the explanations were no longer necessary. The old man's face broke into a smile as suddenly the world jumped back into focus.

'*That* Carla! Why didn't you say so?' He held a bony hand out to her. 'How wonderful to see you, my dear! Come over and sit here on the bed.'

With a smile, Carla did so, laying her bag of fruit on the nearby armchair and casting a curious glance across at Jedd. There'd been something inexpressibly affectionate and caring about the way he'd performed that little service with the spectacles. And now, as he continued to watch the old man, the look on his face—fiercely protective, yet utterly tender—was almost making her feel as though she was looking at a complete stranger.

She'd always been aware that Jedd got on well with Jasper, but here she was witnessing an intensity of feeling she frankly would never have believed he was capable of.

Perhaps he felt her watching eyes, for all at once he turned to look at her, the warmth in his expression instantly draining away. In its place was a warning. Tread carefully, it told her.

The sudden harshness in his face sent a shiver through Carla's heart. She'd been absolutely right. He really did believe that she was here to try and cold-bloodedly profit from the old man. It was monstrous. She snatched her gaze away and turned to the figure in the bed.

'It's wonderful to see you, too…and looking much better than I'd expected.' For in spite of his ghostly pallor and the pinched look about his cheeks his eyes still held the hint of a sparkle. Whatever the doctors and everyone else might be saying, it was plain that he hadn't quite given up yet.

With a sense of relief, she leaned forward and took his hand. Maybe, after all, there was a glimmer of hope.

'Well, what a surprise you turning up like this—and after all this time.' Jasper was shaking his head. 'Quite amazing, isn't it, Jedd?'

'It certainly is.'

'Actually, it was pure chance.' Before Jedd could say more—and possibly blacken her name in the process!— Carla quickly cut in, then went on to explain what had actually brought her to the area—about the ad she'd responded to and how she'd arrived only a couple of days ago. 'But I didn't know till yesterday, when Annie told me, that you were ill. Naturally, I had to come and see you straight away.'

She was aware that this explanation was partly for Jedd's sake. As she spoke, she glanced across at him, half angrily, half imploringly. I swear, her eyes promised him, that's the absolute truth.

There was no softening in the dark gaze. He just looked back at her unblinkingly, making it very plain that she was wasting her time. Damn you, she thought, turning away again impatiently. Though what on earth had made her think there was any point in trying to persuade him? He appeared to be capable of some finer

feelings towards his uncle, but where she was concerned
he was made of pure unbending steel.

'Well, I'm very glad you did.' Jasper was speaking
again. 'What could possibly be better for an old man in
poor health than a visit from a beautiful and charming
young girl like you?' As she laughed at that, he added,
'And you're going to be working at the centre? You'll
enjoy it. It's an excellent place. They do wonderful work
there.'

'I'm enjoying it already.' Carla squeezed his hand.
'And you're right. It really is a very special place.'

Jasper nodded. 'I've never actually managed to make
a visit.' He made a face. 'I've been stuck in this
wretched bed for too long. But Jedd's told me all about
it. He's very involved with it, you see.'

'Jedd? With the Starship Centre?' Carla gaped in disbelief. Part of her wanted to laugh at the very idea. Part
of her was horrified at what it would mean if it were
true.

Oh, no. Heaven forbid. She had a sudden horrible vision of him spying on her in the playground, sitting in
on lessons, finding all sorts of little ways to make her
life difficult, and she was aware of a crumbling sensation
inside her. How could she continue to work there if he
really was involved?

She turned to look at him again, trying to hide her
dismay, and, in pretty much the same words he'd used
to her the other day, told him, 'Good heavens, I wouldn't
have thought that was your sort of thing!'

He smiled, clearly guessing at the secret panic that
had filled her. 'I see you like the idea,' he purred. Then,
with a shake of his head, he turned to the figure in the

bed. 'You exaggerate, Uncle. I'm not really involved. I just take a bit of an interest, that's all.'

Carla sagged with relief and let out the breath she'd been holding. Talk about a deeply worrying moment! Though she was crazy, of course. It definitely wasn't his sort of thing, and his claim that he took an interest was probably a load of nonsense. Unless, of course, he had a good reason for doing so.

'You're going to be working alongside young Annie, then?'

As Jasper spoke again, Carla turned away gratefully to answer him. 'That's right, and we'll actually be working pretty closely. For most of the time, I'll be sharing her office. And I must say I'm looking forward to it. I really like her a lot.'

Jasper nodded. 'She's a lovely girl. Everyone loves Annie.'

In a flash, the penny dropped. Carla smiled to herself. Now she understood, though she really ought to have guessed anyway. The most obvious explanation for Jedd's alleged interest in the centre had to be that he had a fancy for its pretty, crop-haired principal!

She slid him a curious glance. So, were he and Annie lovers, or hadn't things reached that stage yet? She recalled her friend's disappointment the other day when she'd returned to the car park to find him gone. Was the poor girl in love with him? She felt a protective rush inside her. Being in love with a difficult, opinionated man like Jedd Hunter would definitely be no picnic!

Jasper broke into these thoughts. 'So, come on, Carla, tell us what you've been up to since last time we saw you. Are you still enjoying life up in London?'

'Yes, I am. Very much.'

Carla smiled to herself again. Her life as an underpaid schoolteacher with a London mortgage was undoubtedly a far cry from what he imagined—and very, very different from what it had been two years ago. Then, between her PR job and Nicholas's connections, it had been a constant, breathless round of receptions and parties, theatres and restaurants and weekends at posh country houses. An extremely glitzy time. Jedd had been quite right about that. These days, by contrast, the only luxuries she could afford were the occasional trip to a cinema or a takeaway from her local curry house!

Still, she wasn't complaining. She was much happier now. Since she'd gone back to teaching, it was as though her life had some real purpose. She knew that the job she was doing was worthwhile.

'I'm at a school near Holloway Road,' she continued. 'The kids there are great.' Then, seeing that the old man was interested in what she was saying, she went on to recount a little of her daily life, throwing in a couple of amusing stories to make him smile.

As she spoke, she kept her eyes fixed exclusively on Jasper. Not once did she as much as flick a glance across at Jedd. Why should she subject herself to that hostile grey gaze? But she knew he was listening. Listening and dissecting. She could feel his eyes boring through the back of her skull.

He's trying to psyche me out, but he won't succeed. As far as I'm concerned, he doesn't exist.

After a while, she became aware that the old man was growing tired. She leaned forward and took his hand. 'I think it's time—' she began, about to go on to say that

she would go now and let him rest. But she never finished the sentence. She nearly jumped from the bed in
fright as, like some bad-tempered beast suddenly erupt-
ing from its lair, Jedd rose to his feet, impatiently pushing back his chair.

'That's enough!' he announced. 'You're wearing the
old man out. I insist that you say your goodbyes now
and leave.'

'I was about to do just that, so there's no need to
insist.' Angry at his tone, Carla spun round to face him.
'I don't need you acting as my watchdog!' she snapped.

'Good.' He held her eyes. 'But if I was acting as anyone's watchdog I can assure you it was my uncle's. He's
the one who needs protecting.'

Carla felt herself flush. She looked back at him
squarely. 'I agree. But not from me. I have only his best
interests at heart.'

She turned away before she could see the look of dis-
missal that would provoke and got up from the bed, still
holding the old man's hand, pleased to see that he'd
momentarily drifted off to sleep and had been quite unaware of that angry exchange. But, feeling the bed move,
he opened his eyes now. He blinked at her and frowned.
'You're not leaving already?'

'Yes, I'm afraid I have to. And, anyway, you need a
rest. But I'll come back and see you again soon if you'd
like that.'

Her stomach tightened as she said it. To Jedd's suspicious ears, that had probably sounded like a deliberate
provocation. But it had been nothing of the sort. She'd
just said what she felt. It would be a pleasure to come

over whenever she had a couple of hours free. And if Jedd had a problem with that it was really just too bad.

Jasper nodded in response. 'I'd like that very much.' He smiled. 'Feel free to come any time you like. Just pick up the phone and have a word with Jedd and he'll see to it that there's a boat available to bring you across. We don't want you having to rely on the ferries.'

He paused and cast a glance at the silent presence behind Carla. 'You wouldn't mind doing that, would you, Jedd?'

There was a tense second of silence before Jedd gave his answer. Carla suppressed a wicked smile, imagining the look on his face. It must be taking all his will-power not to strangle her on the spot!

But when he spoke his tone was calm. 'Of course I wouldn't mind. I shall enjoy taking charge of Miss Roberts' visits to the island.'

Carla spun round to look into his composed, smiling face. What exactly did he mean by that? It sounded most worrying. She had a nasty suspicion she'd just been caught in a trap.

Not quite, though. Forewarned was forearmed, after all.

'How kind of you,' she told him, forcing a light smile. What she was actually thinking was, You'll be doing no such thing! I'll be taking great care to keep you well out of the picture...so don't hold your breath waiting for any phone calls. I much prefer to take the ferry!

She kissed the old man goodbye and headed for the door—which Jedd was already holding open for her. But just as it seemed he was about to follow her outside, in answer to her secret prayers, the old man called out to him, 'Jedd, just a minute before you go...'

Carla breathed with relief. Thank you, Jasper. You're a friend! Then, as Jedd about-turned and disappeared back into the room, she headed swiftly along the corridor, making for the stairs.

At the top, she glanced at her watch. It was later than she'd thought. What a pity. There wouldn't be time, after all, for that cup of coffee and a chat with Henrietta— not if she was to catch the next ferry back. Which she absolutely had to do. Her class would be waiting.

I'd better go and find Henrietta and tell her I'm sorry, she decided. We can have our little get-together next time I'm over.

Almost running, she reached the foot of the stairs, then stopped. The only problem now was where to find Henrietta. The hall was deserted. There was no one to ask. She glanced round with a perplexed frown, then an idea came to her. Maybe she'd decided to wait for her in the main drawing room, which was situated, if she remembered correctly, beyond the double doors at the end of the hall.

The doors stood half open. Carla hurried towards them. 'Henrietta!' she called out. 'Henrietta! Are you there?'

When no one answered, she gave a couple of quick taps to announce her presence, then stepped forward and poked her head inside the room.

'Henrietta! It's Carla. I'm afraid I've got to leave now.'

'In that case, you'd better go. Henrietta's not here.'

Out of nowhere, Jedd had suddenly appeared before her, making her leap about five feet in the air.

CHAPTER FOUR

'WHERE the devil did you spring from?' Carla stepped back, catching her breath. 'And what do you mean by jumping out at me like that?'

Jedd was standing just inside the drawing-room doorway and it was perfectly plain from his look of amusement that the last thing on his mind was offering an apology.

He raised mocking black eyebrows. 'I wasn't aware of jumping out at you. I heard you calling for Henrietta and came to tell you she's not here.'

How uncommonly civil! Carla regarded him suspiciously. 'How did you get here anyway? I didn't see you come down the stairs.'

'Ah. So you were keeping a watch out for me, were you?' His eyes scanned her face. He knew very well that she'd been hoping to escape without having to endure another encounter. 'Well, the fact that you didn't see me can be easily explained. I didn't use the main stairs. I came down the back way.'

'So you could surprise me, no doubt. So you could leap out and give me a heart attack.'

'And why would I want to do that?' He feigned shock at the very idea. 'That would be most inconvenient. It would create all sorts of bother.'

Like the hassle of having to phone for an ambulance, for example. He didn't have to say it. She knew what he was getting at. Her lying stricken at his feet would simply be an inconvenience. Had he been anyone else Carla would probably just have laughed, but with anyone else she'd have known it was only a joke. With Jedd, despite his smile, you couldn't really be sure.

He was continuing. 'The reason I came down the back stairs was actually because I was hoping to avoid you. I'd no idea you were about to start prowling about the house.'

'I wasn't prowling about. I was looking for Henrietta.'

'Well, you were wasting your time. Henrietta's not here.'

'Might I ask how you happen to know that?' Carla didn't believe him. He was just fobbing her off, trying to get her to leave.

'Very simple. I know because I know Henrietta. Seeing as I was around, she decided to make herself scarce.'

'And why would she do that?'

'I'm afraid you'll have to ask her.' He fixed her with an impassive look as Carla peered back at him, wondering what he'd done to poor Henrietta to make her so anxious to keep out of his way.

Then he smiled an amused smile. 'But I can assure you she's not here. Apart from the reason I've already given you, I know this is the case because on my way downstairs I glanced out the window and happened to notice that her car had gone.'

Carla glared at him. Was that the truth? Before she could decide, he went on, 'You shouldn't be so surprised. Surely you must have noticed that she wasn't exactly overjoyed when she opened the door and saw me sitting there at Uncle Jasper's bedside?'

That makes two of us. Carla remembered her own sense of horror when she'd stepped across the threshold and suddenly spotted him. He definitely possessed a very special talent for striking dismay into the hearts of those who knew him.

With the exception of Annie, of course. The thought jumped into her head. Foolish, trusting Annie had allowed herself to be ensnared by that dark, brooding physical allure he exuded. She was playing a losing game, of course—Jedd would never make her happy— though Carla understood how easily it could happen. She, too, had once briefly fallen under his spell.

She pushed that thought away and tilted her head at him. 'Well, I can't say I blame Henrietta for disappearing. She obviously prefers to try and avoid trouble.'

'Unlike you.'

'What do you mean?'

'You chose to ignore my advice.' As she frowned, he added, 'About coming to the island.'

'Ah, so that was advice, was it?' Carla smiled a scathing smile. 'Funny. At the time, it sounded more like a warning.'

'Yet you still chose to ignore it.' He narrowed his eyes at her. 'It would appear that, unlike my cousin, you rather enjoy a bit of trouble.'

'Not at all. I just don't believe in giving in to bullies.' She fixed him with a level look. 'You'd no right to forbid me. I knew Jasper would be pleased to see me and, as you saw for yourself, I was right.'

While she was speaking, he'd turned and taken a few steps into the drawing room. Beside a mahogany drum table he now came to a halt and, swivelling round to face her again, leaned his jeans-clad hip against it. A shaft of light from one of the windows fell across him for a moment, illuminating the lines of his strong, chiselled features. For an instant, it was the bronze head of some warrior of old.

Carla was aware of a quick, warm stirring inside her. A flashback into the past. That episode on the boat. She could see again the lightning that lit up the sky around them, feel the charge of his rain-drenched skin against her own and the tumbling, wild excitement as he swept her into his arms.

The power of the memory shocked her. She banished it at once and, in the process, found herself thinking of Annie again and wondering if the two of them were lovers, after all. But what did *that* have to do with anything? She crushed that thought too. Then, almost gratefully, she became aware that Jedd was speaking again.

'So, tell me…all that stuff you were saying to my uncle…about how your life's so hard these days—all work and no play—was it actually on the level or just a device to whip up sympathy?'

'You mean in the hope that he might feel so sorry for me that he'd decide to present me with a nice fat cheque or something?' Carla fixed him with an accusing look. 'I know that's what you're thinking. And, though I'm sorry you believe it, I haven't the slightest intention of trying to convince you you're mistaken. I absolutely refuse to stoop to that level.'

It was the same way she'd felt two years ago and nothing had altered, in spite of those brief doubts she'd had that perhaps she'd been too proud. The fact was she *was* that proud. It was the way she was made.

She saw a look cross his eyes. He seemed to study her for a moment. He's probably telling himself that was just a roundabout confession of guilt, she decided. Well, it couldn't be helped. Let him think what he liked.

'Besides,' she continued when he remained silent, still watching her, 'you're wrong to suppose that I consider my life hard. Maybe to you it sounds hard, but I'm more than satisfied. I'm poorer than I once was, but much happier, believe it or not.'

'You don't miss the high life, then?' He cocked his head and raised an eyebrow. Then he treated her to a slow, openly disbelieving smile. 'Forgive me if I have to say that comes as a surprise. It appeared to be such an essential part of you last time we met.'

'Did it? Well, it never was.'

Still, she could appreciate that it might have seemed so. She paused, thinking back to that strange period of her life when everything had been upside down and inside out. And for a moment she had to drop her eyes and glance away as she remembered how it had all started, with the death of her beloved mother, a blow that at the time she'd thought she'd never survive. Even now, she was aware of a quick shaft of pain, as though she'd grazed against a scar not properly healed.

Pulling herself free, she raised her eyes again. 'It was just a passing phase. The ''high life'', as you call it, wasn't really me, I'm afraid.'

'No? You were just pretending?'

'Something like that. I can live perfectly well without going to fancy restaurants and first nights. They were never an important ingredient in my life.'

As she said it, it suddenly struck her that he might

think she was trying to get round him. After all, he didn't exactly pursue the high life himself! So she hurriedly added, just to quash any such notion, 'At the same time, I'd have to admit that I enjoyed it.' It had been a taste of a way of life she'd never known before.

Jedd's eyes were still on her, narrowed, probing pin-points. 'So, what you seem to be saying is that there's more than one Carla Roberts…?' He appeared to reflect on this. 'I wonder which is the real one?'

'I suspect you'll never know that.'

Carla fixed him a cool look. Over the past few minutes it had actually crossed her mind that perhaps he could be excused for having so totally misjudged her. But that was sheer nonsense. She might have given the impression of being the type of girl who rather liked her little luxuries, but that hardly gave him the right to assume she was a gold-digger!

She added, 'But I'm sure you're not actually interested in knowing the truth. You're so totally convinced that you've got it all figured out.'

Still leaning against the table, he straightened slightly and, again, for a fleeting moment, his head was bathed in light from the window. He said, 'I think I may have caught a glimpse of the true you once.'

Something shifted inside her. That memory again. She felt herself tense. 'And when might that have been?' But she was faking. She knew he meant on the boat.

Jedd took a step towards her. 'Once, when your defences were down. In a situation like that it's hard to hide who you really are.'

Her heart was beating fast. She was remembering how they'd kissed. The excitement she'd felt. How carried away she'd been. But that hadn't been the real her. He was crazy if he believed that.

He took another step towards her to stand in front of her again. Carla wanted to move away, but her feet were stuck to the floor.

'Anyway…' He smiled down at her. 'It certainly looks as though I'm going to have plenty of opportunity to get acquainted with the true you. It seems we'll be spending quite a bit of time in each other's company.'

'What makes you think that?'

She was trying not to notice how one lock of his hair had fallen down across his forehead. It was so glossy and black, it almost looked wet. If she reached out and touched it it would be cool to the touch.

His eyes scanned her face. 'Oh, I think it's inevitable. You're obviously planning to make regular trips to see my uncle, so I really have no choice but to sit in and keep an eye on you. You say I'm wrong about who you are, but I'd rather not take any chances.'

'Suit yourself.' Carla was aware of a quick flare of anger. But he was fooling himself if he thought she was going to allow him to be her little shadow. As she'd already resolved, there was no way in the world that she'd be letting him know when she planned to come over.

It was as though he'd read her mind. A smile flickered across his face. 'Naturally, of course, I won't be expecting any phone calls. It was naive of the old man even to suggest such a thing.'

He paused, clearly amused by the abrupt shift in her expression and the way two spots of colour had risen in her cheeks. 'But I'll know, nevertheless, the instant you set foot on the island. So don't think for one minute that you'll be able to sneak in.'

Damn him! He'd seen right through her. Carla glared into his face. 'Well, I suppose it's up to you, but I'm really a bit surprised that you've obviously got nothing better to do than play chaperon to me.'

'Oh, I've got plenty better to do. But I consider it a duty.' He paused and stared at her for a moment. 'Besides, I'm sure there'll be compensations.'

He'd been standing very still, but now suddenly he moved. As his hand came up between them, Carla was quite certain that he was about to take hold of her and kiss her. She felt her whole body go limp then grow tense in the same instant. A rush of excitement followed by a sharp thrust of horror. Without stopping to think, she raised her hand to strike him.

She realised immediately she'd been mistaken. He was simply reaching up to push the hair back from his forehead.

Carla stopped, her hand hovering guiltily in mid-air, her embarrassment written plainly in the flaming crimson of her cheeks. I'm crazy, she thought. What's going on in my head? This was almost a replay of what had happened that time on the boat.

Jedd's reaction was to smile. 'Hey, aren't you jumping the gun a bit? Aren't we at least supposed to kiss first before I get the slap across the face?'

'No, we're not!'

She swung away. It was time she got out of here. She'd already made a big enough fool of herself. On legs that felt like paper she began to sprint across the hall. Behind her, she could hear the infuriating sound of Jedd laughing.

But she didn't turn round. Let him laugh if he liked. Who could blame him anyway? In his shoes she'd be laughing too. She snatched the door open, plunged down the steps and didn't stop running till she'd reached the end of the driveway.

How could she have done that? Talk about giving yourself away! She headed down the winding road that led to the jetty. And what was wrong with her anyway? Was her brain going soft? Why did everything suddenly remind her of that episode on the boat? She just had to look at him and she was back in the storm, reliving how it had felt to be wrapped in his arms.

Stop it, she chastised herself. You're starting again! Shaking herself, she snatched a quick glance at her watch—and instantly all thoughts of storms and things were wiped from her head. Horrors! She'd blown it. She'd never catch the ferry now. It was due to leave in about two seconds' time!

All the same, she started to run again, praying it might set off late. If she missed it, she'd really drop Annie in a mess.

By the time she rounded the corner and came in sight of the quay, she was scarcely able to breathe for the stitch in her side. But her prayers had been answered. The ferry was still there. Waving frantically to catch the pilot's attention, she tore down the cobbled approach to the jetty. She'd die if he were to cast off now, when she was almost there!

But as she staggered towards the boat he was holding out his hand to her.

'Come along, miss,' he invited 'Now sit you down
and catch your breath.'

With a grateful smile, Carla collapsed into the one
remaining empty seat. 'Thank you,' she mouthed. She
was quite incapable of speech.

The pilot glanced at her with a smile as his mate began to cast off. 'You didn't have to rush like that, you
know, young lady,' he told her. 'I wouldn't have minded
waiting for you for another few minutes.'

Carla frowned at him. He seemed to be saying that
he'd already been waiting for her, yet how could he
when he hadn't even known she was coming? But, as
the mate wound up the gangway, he went on to explain.

''Mr. Jedd phoned down to ask me to hang on for
you. He said you'd just left the house and would probably be about fifteen minutes.' He took the wheel as the
boat began to slip away from the jetty. 'Naturally, I was
only too happy to oblige.'

Carla responded with a stiff smile. She ought to feel
grateful, but she didn't. Couldn't the wretched man keep
his nose out of her business even for five minutes?

After he'd made his quick phone call to the ferry pilot,
Jedd went back to Jasper's room and stood watching him
from the foot of the bed. Good. He was still sleeping.
Sleep was what he needed most.

He looked down at the tired old face, almost as pale
as the linen pillows, and felt a huge surge of protective
love rise up inside him. Carla's visit had done no harm.
Quite the contrary, in fact. For a while, she'd brought
the sparkle back to his eyes. Maybe, after all, it wasn't

such a bad thing that she'd be coming over to visit him from time to time.

A wry smile touched his lips. And, to be perfectly honest, old Jasper wasn't the only one who got a boost when she was around!

He knew he was a fool, but there was just something about her... Partly the way she looked—that lovely face with those deep blue eyes—though there was actually a great deal more to it than that. She seemed to radiate an inner energy. There was a brightness in her that drew him. And she had this quick, unexpected sense of humour that never failed to make him smile. There was no denying it. She got to him somehow.

As he felt a flicker of remembered excitement deep inside, his mind switched back to that time on the boat. It should never have happened, of course. She'd been Nicholas's girl then. But the craving he'd felt for her had been too strong to resist. And she'd felt something, too—or at least she had seemed to—in spite of that ardour-cooling slap in the face. He'd often thought he wouldn't mind a repeat of that episode—though, naturally, with a rather more satisfactory ending! And now that she was back... Well, who knew what might happen?

He felt a quick twinge of guilt. He shouldn't be having such thoughts. Blanking them out, he glanced down at his watch. Actually, what he ought to do right now was phone Annie. She'd be wondering where he'd got to, for he'd promised last night that he'd drop round at the centre to see her after lunch today—but, of course, with Carla showing up, he'd had to forget about that.

He frowned. Maybe he could fix up something with

Annie for tomorrow, though visits to the centre were going to be a bit awkward now. The other summer recruits most likely wouldn't give it a second thought, but Carla would soon start to wonder what was going on if she saw him turning up there every other day—which, recently, was more or less what had been tending to happen. So since he'd no wish for his private affairs to come under scrutiny, it might be wise to find another venue for his encounters with Annie.

The figure in the bed stirred.

Jedd stepped forward and bent over him. 'Are you okay, Uncle? Is there anything you need?' But the old man just sighed and went back to sleep.

Straightening, Jedd paused to watch him for a moment. He looked so frail and vulnerable lying there in the big oak bed. Don't worry, he told him silently. I'll look after you.

He frowned to himself, abruptly sobered by that thought. If anything actually were to develop between him and Carla, naturally it would have to be strictly for amusement. In spite of all those clever, beguiling things she'd been saying about how he didn't really know who she was, the fact was he did and he'd be crazy to forget it. At times, the things he knew about her were hard to believe. But he'd been fooled once before and he'd be wise not to forget that.

With a sigh, he turned away. So he'd just enjoy what came along and take care that it didn't turn into anything serious.

At the doorway he paused to cast a last glance at Jasper, then, satisfied, he headed down the corridor to phone Annie.

CHAPTER FIVE

THAT night, Carla had a dream. She was back on the boat two years ago, and the whole thing was so vivid it was as though it was happening all over again.

It had been an act of contrariness to go out alone in the boat in the first place. The main reason she'd done it was that Jedd had said not to. For by that stage—a week and a half into her holiday—he was at the top of the list of her least favourite people.

'You're not experienced enough to handle the boat by yourself,' he warned her. 'If something went wrong, you wouldn't know what to do. Wait till Larry or one of the boys can go with you.' Larry was his right-hand man on the estate. 'For heaven's sake, you don't have to go to-day.'

'I want to go today and I can handle the boat perfectly. I've already had a couple of lessons from Larry. Besides, we're talking about a little motorboat,' she added scoffingly. 'It's not exactly the *Queen Elizabeth* I'm planning to go off with.'

Jedd shook his head at that and turned away impatiently. 'Okay, then. Suit yourself. I won't try to stop you. But if you get into trouble don't expect me to come and rescue you.'

That was a joke! Carla laughed at his back. 'Don't worry, that's the last thing I'd expect. Since when were you the knight in shining armour type?'

Not that there was any danger of her needing his help anyway. And, if anything did happen, she was a pretty strong swimmer.

So, that afternoon, while Jasper was taking his nap, she went down to the private marina and took the boat—just as the old man had said she could do any time she liked. It was a warm day, though not quite as hot as it had been, with a few fluffy clouds scudding across the sky. She climbed aboard, tucking her long hair under her peaked cap.

'You've got plenty of gas,' Pete, the young marina assistant, told her as he untied the mooring rope and tossed it in beside her. 'So you can have yourself a nice long trip if you feel like it.'

'Good. I think that's exactly what I'll do.'

Carla smiled at him. She'd already decided to sail to Gull Point, on the other side of the island. 'It's breathtaking,' Jasper had told her. 'Rugged and wild. In my book, some of the most beautiful scenery in the world.'

She got the engine going in one and, with a quick wave to Pete, began to negotiate her way out of the marina. And as she sat at the wheel, feeling rather pleased with herself, she smiled. In addition to all her other heinous failings, Jedd Hunter clearly believed she was a bit of a dope if he thought she was incapable of managing a small motorboat on her own! Insufferable man. She'd show him just how wrong he was!

From what she'd been told, her journey would take about forty-five minutes. Carla settled back to enjoy it, rather savouring being on her own as the little boat cut through the sparkling blue waves. Not that she was really alone at that stage. There were other craft about, though they grew fewer and fewer as she headed for the west coast. Then, at last, there were none and she felt like the queen of the open sea!

Jasper hadn't been exaggerating. Gull Point was stupendous. As she came round a rocky promontory and suddenly saw it all spread out, she let out a whoop of astonished delight. A tumbling cascade of shrubby green cliff face met the sea in a huge leaping froth of cream foam. Then, further on, where the cliffs dropped back behind the shoreline, gentler waves caressed a silver ribbon of sand.

That was where Carla headed, making use of a rocky outcrop to moor the boat safely before swimming ashore. Then she stretched out on the sand, grinning to herself. Just imagine! She had this paradise all to herself!

It was half an hour or so later that she decided to take a walk. The sun had gone in a bit and the breeze had turned cool. She stood up, slipped on her trainers and pulled on her cap. She'd go and explore the other side of the bay.

Afterwards, Carla would have trouble explaining to herself why it was that she didn't heed the signs. By the time she'd got less than halfway across the bay, the sky had noticeably darkened and the wind was gusting a bit. But she carried on regardless to where the cliffs closed in again. And by then she was aware that it had started to rain.

Still, a few drops of water wouldn't do her any harm and, anyway, it was bound to pass soon. But, as she headed back to where she'd started, she was walking faster than before and by the time she got there she was almost running. The sky had opened, the rain was coming down in torrents and, off in the distance, she could hear the sound of thunder.

What to do? She stood at the sea's edge, her hair dripping round her shoulders, and peered out to where she'd tethered the boat. Waves were crashing all around it, lifting it up, dragging it down. She felt her first small clench of fear. What would she do if it capsized? Or, worse, if it broke loose from its mooring and was swept away?

She'd be marooned here and no one even knew where she was. She could die of thirst or starve to death long before she was found.

Frowning, she searched the sky for a reassuring crack of light. But the heavens had turned black, the thunder was getting closer and the angry grey clouds were hanging so low now that they seemed to merge with the pewter-coloured sea. It wasn't going to get better. It was going to get worse.

The only thing to do was stay put till the storm passed. But what about the boat? It was bucking like a drunken stallion. If the rope didn't snap it was almost bound to break loose. When she'd fixed it she hadn't been expecting weather like this.

And the boat was essential. Without it, she was lost. On an impulse, she pulled off her trainers and cap and threw herself into the buffeting waves. She must bring the boat inshore, right onto the beach, if she could manage it. It was her lifeline. Somehow, she had to keep the boat safe.

She was just in time. As she swam towards it, she could see that the mooring was coming loose. Another few seconds and the boat would have been lost. She reached out to grab the rope—and that was when it happened. A massive great wave suddenly caught her from behind, knocking her sideways, forcing her under. When she surfaced again, gasping, a few seconds later, the boat had been carried out of her reach.

Damn! Fighting the currents, she headed after it. And finally, in spite of the waves that kept separating them, with a superhuman lunge, she managed to grab hold of the side.

'Got you!'

Gritting her teeth, she hung on for dear life. Then, taking advantage of a sudden swelling wave, she hoisted herself up and scrambled aboard. She was so far out to sea now it would be better to drive the boat back. Then, once she reached the shallows, she'd tow it the rest of the way.

She turned towards the shore to get her bearings, then stopped, eyes searching, feeling her stomach turn to ice. The island had vanished as surely as though it had fallen down a hole.

Don't panic, she told herself, forcing herself to breathe slowly. Just get the engine started and wait for the next flash of lightning. That'll show you where you ought to be headed. She stumbled over to the cockpit and pushed the starter button.

Nothing.

She tried again, then a third time, then a fourth. In the end, she must have tried fifty times at least. But it was hopeless. She sank down on the seat to catch her breath, suddenly aware of the water that was sloshing round her ankles and of the fact that every inch of her was shivering with cold. And for the first time she actually thought it. Oh, God, I'm going to die!

Well, if she was, she'd die fighting! She jumped to her feet and started baling out water with her bare hands.

'Carla!'

She froze. She was going crazy. Hearing voices. She went back to scooping out water. But then it came again.

'Carla! Are you there? Carla, can you hear me?'

Holding her breath, she peered into the storm. Was there really someone there? Surely it wasn't possible? But then she heard the voice a third time and it sounded closer now.

'Carla! Are you there? Call back if you can hear me!'

'I can hear you! I can hear you! I'm over here and I'm going under!'

As she yelled back at the top of her lungs, she could see a light flashing. She felt a rush of relief like an explosion inside her. She wasn't going to die! Someone was coming to save her!

'I'm over here! Over here!'

The light was drawing closer and she could make out the dark, fuzzy outline of a small boat. Then, gradually, the figure aboard came into focus, though the hood of his oilskin jacket almost totally obscured his face. More than likely it was Pete, who'd seen her off from the marina. He was a hero. She'd be grateful to him for the rest of her life.

He was tossing a rope, securing her boat to his. Carla felt like grabbing hold of him, throwing her arms round him and kissing him. 'Thank heavens you've come,' she yelled. 'I really thought I was a goner.'

It was at that moment that he raised his head, so that

the hood fell back from his face. Carla's heart nearly stopped. It wasn't Pete. It was Jedd.

'Give me your hand!'

He was stretching out towards her, his expression as black as the thundering sky at his back. Stiffening, Carla hesitated. Suddenly, climbing into the boat with him seemed a far less appealing option than just staying where she was.

'Give me your hand!' he ordered again, impatience snapping in every syllable. Then, before she had time to do so, he reached forward and grabbed hold of her, plucking her from the icy water that was now halfway up her calves, then propelling her through the air as though she were weightless.

'Maybe you want to hang around and drown,' he barked as he dumped her unceremoniously onto the deck behind him, 'but I'm afraid I'm not feeling particularly suicidal today.'

More like homicidal! Carla staggered and fought to keep her balance. It was perfectly clear that he was as mad as a snake at having been forced to come out after her.

'Put this on. Quickly!'

He was thrusting something at her. A yellow waxed jacket similar to his own. Carla took it and struggled obediently to pull it over her head, but her fingers were so numb she could barely keep hold of it. Oh, lord! she thought. Any moment now the wind would snatch it away.

'Come here. Hold still. Let me do it for you!' Jedd pulled her towards him and yanked the jacket over her head, almost dislocating her arms as he thrust them into the sleeves. 'Now sit down over there,' he commanded, steering her backwards till she collided with the bench and went down with a thud. 'And just keep out of my way until I can get us out of here.'

Carla glared at his back as he adjusted the tow rope, then, revving the engine, set the boat in motion again. It was totally perverse, but she couldn't help thinking that she'd have preferred to have been left to take her chances on her own. The thought of being in his debt really stuck in her craw.

Over the past few minutes the storm had got much worse. Shafts of jagged lightning were tearing the sky apart, the waves seemed more like vast, rolling mountains and the boat was plunging about like a bronco at a rodeo.

'Surely you're not planning to try and get back home in these conditions?' Carla had to yell to make herself heard above the thunder. 'It's madness. We'll never make it. You'd have done better not to come.'

He flashed her a look. 'Thanks for the vote of confidence. I'll remember that next time and save myself the trouble.'

'Don't worry, there isn't going to be a next time. We're both going to end up at the bottom of the ocean.'

Even as she said it, Carla felt thoroughly ashamed of herself. How could she make such an ungrateful remark? She huddled into her waxed jacket and dropped her eyes away as he turned back to the controls again as though she weren't there. He was a pig but, for heaven's sake, he was trying to save her life!

And, besides, there was absolutely no point in griping. She was in his hands now, for better or for

QUALITY CHECK LIST

Upholstery Inspected by:

Cushions Inspected by:

Packing Inspected by:

worse…though that, she decided, was an ungenerous thought too. In her heart she no longer felt any fear at all. Somehow, he'd get them out of this. She was absolutely sure of it. She'd been sure of it from the minute she'd looked into his face.

The next quarter of an hour or so was like a roller-coaster ride. Eyes closed, Carla hugged herself, trying to get warm, for her entire shivering body felt like a block of ice. Even if we do get back in one piece, I'm going to die of hypothermia, she kept thinking.

But, suddenly, the wind seemed to have miraculously dropped and, beneath them, the waves had grown inexplicably still. Carla opened her eyes just as she heard Jedd say, 'We're here.'

'Where?' She squinted into the semidarkness. Surely it wasn't possible that they'd got back already? 'What do you mean we're here? Where are we?' she wanted to know.

'We'll be safe here till the storm passes. We're out of its way now.'

He was switching off the engine and tying the boat to a huge rock that loomed above them like a vast vaulted wall. Bewildered, Carla stared about her, then suddenly she understood. They were bobbing about in the mouth of a large cave.

'As you so rightly pointed out, we'd never have made it back.' There was a note of mocking amusement in his voice that told her this was where he'd planned on coming all along. 'So we'll just sit tight here till the storm blows itself out.'

Carla looked at him, wanting to apologise, but something inside her rebelled. Her jaw seemed to clench, making it impossible to get the words out. You're being a jerk, Carla, she told herself, but the next instant she was glad.

'So, why weren't you wearing your life-jacket? That was a bit damned stupid!' Jedd seated himself opposite her, peeling back his hood as he spoke. 'What the hell do you think they put these things in boats for? They're not just there for decoration, you know.'

Carla glared at him. How dared he talk to her as though she were an imbecile? Though, to be honest, all at once that was precisely what she felt like. 'I didn't know where it was. I didn't even know there was one.'

'Surely Larry told you the first time you took the boat out?' The narrowed dark eyes bit impatiently into her. 'It's his job to explain such things and I'd be most surprised if he didn't.'

Yes, she was an imbecile. It was all coming back to her. Larry had told her, but she hadn't paid much attention. It hadn't seemed like anything she needed to know.

'I forgot,' she confessed, feeling about two inches tall.

'You forgot?' His eyebrows soared. 'You were in the middle of a storm and you forgot the small detail that there were life-jackets on board?'

'Yes.' Did he really have to rub it in like this? 'I'm afraid that's what happened. I just didn't think.'

'I suppose you also didn't think that it might be a good idea to use the flares—to signal your position to whoever might come looking for you? If it hadn't been for a particularly vivid flash of lightning, I might never have managed to locate you.'

Carla felt herself blush. That had slipped her mind too, for of course Larry had also explained about the flares.

She cast a mutinous look at Jedd. 'I didn't expect anyone to come looking for me. Not in a storm like this. It never crossed my mind.'

'So you didn't forget about the flares? You just decided not to use them?'

He knew that wasn't the case, of course. He was just having a go at her. But, in spite of that, Carla was aware that all her hostility had abruptly melted. It really hadn't crossed her mind, not even for a split second, that anyone might actually brave the storm to come and look for her. But Jedd had. He'd risked his life to save her and, instead of making his task easier, she'd made it more difficult by failing to carry out a pretty basic procedure. Everyone knew you were supposed to use flares when you were in distress.

She felt a rush of burning shame. 'I'm sorry,' she blurted out. 'I'm really sorry. I didn't think. I know it was stupid of me.' She could hear her voice cracking, feel a tightness in her throat. 'I acted like an idiot. I'm afraid I just panicked.'

As she finished, her control broke and she burst into tears.

It was the release of all that tension that had been burning a hole inside her. Those terrifying moments when she'd been sure she was going to die. The relief of being saved. The resentment that it was Jedd. The guilt. The defensiveness. It was too much to hold in.

'Hey, there's no need for that.' Suddenly, he'd come to sit beside her, slipping an apologetic arm round her shoulders. 'I didn't mean to upset you. I know you've had a fright. It's just your welfare I'm thinking of. You could have wound up dead.'

'I'm sorry. I really am.' She couldn't stop apologising now! 'I'm not normally that stupid. I just wasn't thinking straight.'

'That's okay. Don't worry about it.' He gave her a gentle squeeze. 'And it all ended well, so let's just forget it. You didn't fall overboard, so you didn't need the life-jacket, and I found you in the end, even without the flares.'

With his free hand he twisted her chin round to look at him and brushed away a tear with the flat of his thumb. He smiled. 'At least next time you'll know what to do.'

'I hope there's never a next time. That was the worst experience ever.'

As she looked at him, a shaft of lightning lit up the sky behind him, so that, suddenly, all the shadows fell away from his face. His hair was plastered to his head, falling in wet curls over his forehead, and there were droplets of rainwater glistening on his lashes. She felt a thrust of desire and a sudden fierce awareness of the strength of the arm that was still wrapped round her shoulders. And, all at once, she dared not move. Confusion rushed through her. Should she pull away from his embrace or simply pretend she hadn't noticed?

For there was a look in the grey eyes that was deeply unsettling. A warmth and a gentle humour she'd never seen before—plus something else as well that disturbed her a great deal more. A hungry, smouldering fire that seemed to leap out and scorch her.

Next instant, they were plunged into semi-darkness once again. Carla tensed, hopelessly aware of the physical contact that, only a couple of minutes ago, had felt quite innocent and unthreatening, but now seemed positively loaded with worrying possibilities. It felt like sitting on top of a loudly ticking bomb.

Brusquely, with the backs of her hands, she wiped away her tears. 'I'm sorry about that. I don't know what came over me.' Clearing her throat, she gave a nervous little laugh. Maybe now he'd remove his arm.

He didn't. 'Don't be silly. You've had a pretty hairy experience.' Very softly, his fingers caressed the top of her arm.

As excitement flared through her, Carla tensed even more, though she'd stopped even pretending that she wished he'd take his arm away. Instead, what she was longing for was the courage to relax against it.

There was a silence. His embrace seemed to tighten a little. She felt a sweet, hungry jolt of pleasure inside her, but still couldn't summon the audacity just to go along with it. He must feel as though he'd got his arm wrapped round a lump of wood, she thought.

Out of nervousness, she broke the silence. 'What made you come looking for me anyway? I mean, what made you think I might have got into trouble?'

'When the storm broke, Pete came and told me you hadn't got back yet. There was obviously a risk, so I decided to try and find you.'

He made it sound so straightforward, but that was probably how it had happened. She could imagine him setting off without a moment's hesitation—not because it was her, of course, but because that was how he did things. She felt a quick, warm flicker of admiration.

'But how did you know where to come? I could have gone anywhere.'

'I used my judgement.' She sensed his smile, felt him squeeze her arm again. 'Knowing you, there was really only one place you could have gone—to the most remote and dangerous part of the island. So that was where I decided to head for.'

How utterly mortifying! Was she really that transparent? He'd probably even guessed she'd gone there partly to defy him!

But perhaps she hadn't been quite as reckless as he believed. She started to explain what had actually happened, how it had originally been her plan to wait the storm out on the beach, how she'd only gone after the boat because it had been in danger of breaking loose.

'If it hadn't been for that, I'd have been perfectly safe. Didn't that occur to you? That I might actually be on dry land, in absolutely no danger at all?'

'It was what I was hoping, but all my instincts were telling me otherwise. And I couldn't take the risk. You see…I didn't want to lose the boat.'

At that precise moment, the entire cave was illuminated by another massive bolt of lightning and Carla could see from his smile that he was joking. 'I've just spent a fortune having it refitted,' he added. As he said it, to her astonishment, he leaned forward and kissed her.

It wasn't meant to be a proper kiss. At least, it didn't seem so at first. It appeared to start out as no more than a flirtatious peck. But at the very last moment, as a violent thunderclap exploded, instead of drawing back again he kept his lips pressed to hers.

Instantly, a wave of warm desire swept through her. As he reached for her and drew her closer, wrapping both his arms round her, she felt her whole body slacken and fall against him at last. All the tension in her had melted. A wonderful, sweet release. With a small sigh of pleasure, she slid her hands to his shoulders and buried her fingers in his slippery, rain-wet hair.

All at once, it was as though the storm was taking place inside her. As his kiss grew more passionate, tearing at her senses, she clung to him, drowning, soaring, flying, caught in a wild, spinning vortex of excitement. The ticking bomb had finally gone off.

Again the lightning flashed and, as Carla half opened her eyes to look at him, she felt a helpless needle of longing pierce through her. No man, ever before, had made her feel like this.

No man.

Something stirred uncomfortably inside her. She held her breath, her brain whirring. And then she remembered.

Nicholas.

It was like a punch in the face. How could she have forgotten? She tried to pull away.

'Come here. What's the matter?'

Jedd refused to let her go. As she arched her head away from him, he bent to kiss her throat, sending tiny electric pulses skittering across her skin.

It was too hard to resist. With a sigh, she surrendered, shivering with helpless pleasure as his lips again found hers, the need in her leaping like a flame given oxygen. Almost fiercely, she held onto him, hands pressed to the back of his head, fingers tangling in his hair, her whole being alight.

But this was all wrong and it was going out of control. She felt herself stiffen as a sudden panic took hold of her. With a small cry, she wrenched free and slapped him hard across the face.

'Stop it!' she shrieked. 'What the hell do you think you're doing?' She jumped from her seat, frantically backing away from him. 'Have you gone crazy or something? How dare you lay a hand on me?'

Even at that moment she knew how false she must have sounded. As another burst of lightning lit up the sky behind them, she saw his look of scorn and knew she deserved it. If anyone had gone crazy it was her.

But it didn't matter what he thought of her, or what she thought of herself. The only thing that counted was knowing she was safe now. Not from the storm—he'd already saved her from that—but from something she found a hundred times more threatening.

What they'd just been through together had briefly broken down all barriers. Instead of anger and dislike, there'd been closeness and a kind of sympathy. She'd forgotten who he was, what he thought of her, what she thought of him, and had allowed herself to be carried off on a tide of empty, treacherous emotion.

To think what that might have led to turned her insides to sawdust. But the danger had gone. They were enemies again.

That was how it had happened and how Carla relived it now in her dream—a dream so vivid that, as she suddenly jolted back to consciousness, she could almost have sworn she really was back on the boat again.

Her heart was pounding like a hammer, her whole body bathed in sweat. And for a long time she just lay there, catching her breath, asking herself, as she'd done many times over the past two years, exactly what it was that she'd been so afraid of.

CHAPTER SIX

CARLA knew there was no point in trying to go straight back to sleep. Her brain was still spinning, not quite out of the dream yet. So she climbed out of bed and pulled on her dressing gown. She'd go down to the kitchen and get herself a drink. That might help to calm her down.

First, though, she stopped off to look in on Freddie, the difficult little redhead who'd caught her eye in the playground yesterday when he'd got into a bit of an altercation about a ball. Just last night, she'd been awakened by cries coming from one of the bedrooms along the corridor and had gone rushing in to find poor Freddie in the throes of a nightmare. A *real* nightmare, not something silly like she'd just experienced.

It had taken her ages to calm him down. The poor little soul had been in a terrible state. But, eventually, he'd fallen into a deep, peaceful sleep, with her still sitting there at his bedside smoothing his brow and holding his hand. It had been nearly dawn before she'd finally slipped away.

Today, she'd learned from the other children that it wasn't the first time Freddie had had a disturbed night. He often cried out in his sleep, though not as badly as last night. So Carla had decided that, from now on, she'd be keeping a very special eye on him.

But now, as she looked into the bedroom he shared with five other boys, he and the rest of his companions were sleeping like babies. She paused for a moment to watch them, then carried on downstairs.

A bright moon was shining through the uncurtained kitchen window. Without bothering to switch the light on, Carla went straight to the fridge, took a carton of orange juice down from the shelf, poured herself a glass and took a long, refreshing swig. She was just about to shut the fridge door when, to her surprise, she heard a car drawing up in the road outside.

At this hour? How strange. It was after one o'clock. Stepping to the window, she peered across the garden to the tree-lined street beyond the fence. And there, perfectly illuminated by a nearby street lamp, stood a rather familiar-looking Land Rover.

She felt herself stiffen. An anxious jolt in her breast. What could Jedd possibly be doing here at this time of night?

It was at that moment that the passenger door suddenly opened and Annie jumped down onto the pavement. Carla stared in amazement. She'd thought Annie was in bed! And all the while she'd been having a secret tryst with Jedd!

Annie was saying something into the car, then laughing as she slammed the door shut. And there was a jauntiness in her step as she headed for the gate, pausing to give Jedd a final cheerful wave.

As the car accelerated off, Carla moved away from the window. What should she do now? It would be idiotic to try to hide. Annie might very well come into the kitchen. And why should she hide anyway? She hadn't been doing anything wrong!

Though it might look as though she had. Quickly, she

switched the light on. She'd no desire to be taken for some peeping Tom, lurking about suspiciously in the dark!

A moment later, as the front door opened, she poked her head out into the corridor. 'I thought that was you. I was just getting myself some fruit juice.' She smiled a bright smile and held up her glass as proof.

Annie's expression definitely fell a bit. At the end of the corridor, she paused, an oddly defensive look settling on her face. And for a moment she seemed at a total loss as to what to say. 'I went out,' she offered, somewhat feebly, at last.

'Yes, I saw the car.' Inwardly, Carla frowned. Why on earth was Annie acting so strangely? It was nothing to her that she'd been out on the tiles with Jedd! 'Oh, well,' she added, 'I'd better get back to bed.' And she stepped into the corridor, about to head for the stairs.

But then Annie spoke again. 'Jedd phoned unexpectedly, just as I was about to go to bed, and asked if I'd like to join him for a drink.' As she paused, Carla could almost hear the cogs of her brain working. The silly girl was trying to think up some innocent excuse. But why was she bothering? What was she so worried about?

She nodded in response. 'Did you go somewhere nice?'

'Nowhere special. The Partridge Inn. You know, just for a friendly drink.'

Carla knew the Partridge Inn. She'd driven past it once. Just outside St Orvel, it was an old country house hotel with beautiful landscaped gardens and rose-smothered walls. Very olde-worlde and extremely picturesque. By anybody's reckoning, a perfect setting for romance.

A friendly drink, my eye, she thought as something clicked in her brain. So Annie was sleeping with Jedd, after all!

'We just talked about this and that. Nothing important. He was telling me about some plans he's got for the estate.'

She sounded so earnest, as though she was desperate for it to be understood that the meeting had had nothing at all to do with sex, that Carla found herself wondering, Has Jedd sworn her to secrecy? What other reason could there be for this mysterious behaviour?

'It was terribly interesting. He's got some excellent ideas.' Annie paused and gave an elaborate yawn. 'But I'll tell you about it tomorrow. It's time I got to bed.'

Back in her room, Carla climbed between the sheets. Sleep, she told herself as she switched off the light. Just concentrate on that. Don't think of anything else. But as she snuggled down, pulled the covers over her shoulders and closed her eyes all sorts of unruly images were jumping into her head.

Annie in bed with Jedd at the Partridge Inn. Then no more Annie. Suddenly, it was her instead and she was back on the boat with him, her fingers tangling in his hair. He was kissing her. She was kissing him back. Then they were sinking to the deck, warm limbs entwined in a scorching embrace.

Then the boat became a bed, a big four-poster affair, like the ones they would have in the best rooms at the Partridge Inn. And suddenly they were naked together and not just kissing but making love—the passion that possessed them as wild and unbridled as the storm that had raged in the sky overhead.

It wasn't the first time Carla's thoughts had turned crazy like this. For a while, after that summer, it had kept happening all the time, in spite of her frantic efforts to put a stop to it. She'd felt thoroughly ashamed of herself. What was going on? Was she turning into some kind of nymphomaniac?

Maybe she was, she'd decided. After all, look at what she'd done! She'd virtually thrown herself into the arms of a man she didn't even like and who happened to be her boyfriend's cousin. Though at least, during the few remaining days of the holiday, there'd been no shameful repeats, for she'd barely seen Jedd after that. He'd seemed to avoid her as fastidiously as she'd avoided him.

But surely she was being a bit hard on herself? There'd have been no repeats anyway. The only reason that madness had ever happened was the storm. All the drama and raw emotion had unhinged her.

Of course, none of it would have taken place if she'd been more committed to Nicholas. Storm or no storm, it simply wouldn't have been on the cards. But the situation between her and Nicholas had already been pretty shaky. Just a couple of weeks earlier, she'd tried to break things off and had only relented because of the way he'd begged and pleaded. He'd been kind to her in the past and she'd hated to see him hurt.

She shook herself. But why was she thinking about all this now? None of it mattered. It was all in the past and she didn't need to go looking for excuses for what she'd done. After all, it had just been a harmless bit of lunacy.

Impatiently, she turned over. She was obviously over-tired, which was why she'd had that dream earlier and then lapsed into her mad fantasy. So, think of something else, she commanded herself, and kindly go to sleep!

Closing her eyes, she focused her thoughts on the chil-dren and some of the activities that were planned for next day. And it worked. Eventually. About twenty minutes later, she finally drifted off into a peaceful, dreamless sleep.

'Good afternoon. How lovely to see you again.'

'Did you miss me?'

'Of course. It's been absolute hell.' He smiled. 'But I gritted my teeth and carried on.'

Two days later, when Carla stepped through the castle doorway, Jedd was standing waiting for her at the top of the staircase. She peered up at him with annoyance. Quite frankly, she'd have been amazed if he'd failed to keep his threat to sit in on her visits to Jasper, but, ever optimistic, she'd been hoping for a miracle.

'So, how did you know I was here?' She began to climb the stairs, rather hoping he planned to move before she actually reached the top.

'Oh, I have my spies.'

'Yes, I'll just bet you do.'

'I warned you you wouldn't be able to slip past.'

'Don't worry, I remember. I suppose I should feel flattered that you think I'm worth going to all this bother for.' She treated him to an openly false look of concern. 'I just hope I'm not inconveniencing you too much? I'd die of guilt if I thought you'd had to cancel something important.'

His face broke into a smile. 'Yes, I just bet you would.'

He was leaning lightly against the wooden bannister, arms folded across his blue-shirt-clad chest. In their narrow, faded jeans, his long legs appeared endless, the hard thighs seeming to press threateningly against the worn fabric. To her dismay, Carla found herself thinking of the boat again. Instantly, she felt a warm flare of desire.

'But don't worry,' he added, 'nothing could be more important than spending these few precious moments of time with you.'

'My thoughts precisely.' She was almost at the top of the stairs now and he still showed no sign of moving out of her way.

With a frown, she came to a stop two steps below him. 'Excuse me, but do you plan on letting me past? Or would you rather we just stood here and engaged in idle banter?'

He laughed. 'Well, that would be one way of passing the time. And—who knows?—it might be quite enjoyable.'

'No, it wouldn't.' Carla glared at him. 'And it isn't why I came here. I came to see your uncle and I've only got forty minutes.' She glanced irritably at her watch. 'Actually, thirty-seven now.'

'Okay. We'll leave the idle banter to some other time.' He held her eyes for a moment, then, still smiling, turned away and headed along the corridor that led to the old man's room.

Jasper, she was pleased to see, was looking at lot better. There was a touch of warm colour in the thin, papery cheeks today and a highly encouraging light in his eyes—which brightened even more as she walked into the room.

Carla hugged him. 'You're looking great.' Then she took his hands in hers as she seated herself on the edge of the bed.

Jedd positioned himself in the same high-backed chair as before and proceeded to carry out his silent vigil—for he pretty much left the conversation to her and Jasper, really only joining in when the old man addressed him directly.

Well, that's a relief! Carla reflected to herself. It was almost possible to forget he was there!

But then the conversation took a most unfortunate turn.

Jasper had been talking about holidays when he suddenly asked her, 'So, what about you, my dear? When are you planning to take a holiday? You're going to need one after this little stint at the centre.'

'I wouldn't mind one, I must admit, but there'll be no holiday for me, I'm afraid. When I finish at the centre I'll be going straight back to work. And, anyway, holidays aren't really on my agenda these days.'

'Why ever not? You must alter your agenda. Everybody needs a holiday now and then.'

'I know…'

Carla faltered. She was suddenly horribly aware of Jedd. She'd been about to say quite simply that she'd no spare money to spend on holidays, but she knew he'd be bound to misinterpret that. Part of her thought, so what? But another bit of her felt inhibited. She really didn't like being thought of as a gold-digger.

'Maybe I'll manage a weekend somewhere,' she ended lightly.

'A weekend's not enough. Damned thing's over before it's begun. What you need...'

'Uncle, I think what Carla's trying to tell us is that she can't afford to take a holiday.' Suddenly, Jedd spoke, leaning forward in his chair. As Carla swivelled round to look at him, he fixed his eyes on her. 'I'm right, am I not? That is what you were getting at?'

To Carla's complete mortification, she blushed, as though she really were guilty of trying to manipulate the old man's sympathy—which she could guess was precisely what Jedd was thinking.

She looked back at him, annoyed. 'Yes,' she agreed, her tone flinty. 'Since that happens to be the case, I suppose it was.'

'Well, that's no good. No good at all, is it, Jedd?' Suddenly, Jasper was speaking again. 'I reckon we ought to do something about that.'

Carla felt herself go cold as Jedd continued to look at her, one eyebrow raised, head slightly to one side, as though challenging her to go ahead and take it from there. Did he really think that this was what she'd been angling for? Yes, she assured herself sickly, he did.

She took a deep breath and turned round to face the old man again. 'You'll do nothing about it, though it's kind of you to offer.' She smiled as she spoke, but her tone was firm. 'I don't need a holiday. And now let's talk about something else.'

The subject of holidays wasn't mentioned again. And

neither, more crucially, was the dangerous issue of her lack of cash. But Carla was still feeling deeply upset—more than just angry: wounded, too, and confused—when she finally left and headed down to the jetty. She kept trying to tell herself she didn't care what Jedd thought of her. But she did care. It was horrible. And it also made no sense. Where had his abysmal opinion of her come from?

It had to have come from somewhere. It had to have some basis. As she sat on the ferry back to St Orvel, her brain was struggling to come up with an answer. As a character, he was far too rational, far too questioning to turn against her for no reason at all. And he acted as though he knew something. Yet there was nothing to know. It just didn't add up and it was time she got to the bottom of it.

An idea occurred to her. Maybe Henrietta could offer some insights. I'll ask her when I see her tomorrow, she decided. For Henrietta had phoned her at the centre yesterday evening, full of apologies for her abrupt withdrawal the other day and suggesting that they meet up for that chat they'd promised themselves.

'How about tea the day after tomorrow?' she'd proposed. 'But not at the house. Somewhere in town.'

'Fair enough,' Carla had agreed. So they'd arranged to meet at The Griddle, where, according to Henrietta, they made the best scones in town.

Right, Carla decided now as the ferry bumped against the jetty. Tomorrow, over the scones and strawberry jam, let's see if I can pick Henrietta's brains!

In fact, it proved to be a most illuminating meeting, though not in the way that Carla had been hoping, for

Henrietta was unable to throw any light at all on what lay at the root of Jedd's bad opinion of her.

'Heaven knows what it's about. But don't let it worry you. You're not the only one he's got it in for.' She leaned across the table towards Carla and frowned. 'Really, you ought to count yourself lucky that the occasional insult's all you get from him. Just wait till you hear what he's been up to with Nicholas.' And she proceeded to recount a chilling little tale that explained the sudden outbreak of bad blood between her and Jedd.

The following day, when Carla went back to visit Jasper, Jedd was waiting for her at the top of the stairs again. But this time he simply told her, 'Okay, let's go,' and proceeded to lead her along the corridor. Gratefully, Carla followed. After what Henrietta had told her, she didn't feel like indulging in idle conversation with him. Her friend's revelations had shocked her rather a lot.

The old man seemed tired today, so Carla didn't stay long. After less than half an hour, she leaned to kiss the wrinkled cheek. 'I think it's best if you have a rest now. But I'll be back to see you soon.'

On her previous visit, Jedd had remained with his uncle after she left, and as she stepped out into the corridor, closing the door behind her, Carla was praying he'd do the same now. She headed for the stairs, walking fast, almost running. But she'd scarcely got halfway along the corridor when she heard the bedroom door re-open.

'What's the hurry? The ferry doesn't leave for another thirty-five minutes.' As she turned round reluctantly, Jedd was striding towards her. 'There's really no need to go rushing off like that.'

'I wasn't rushing off. I was just leaving, that's all.'

Carla wished she could just ignore him, turn around and keep on going. But something was stopping her. A perverse curiosity to look into his eyes now that she knew what she knew.

She did so. 'Was there something in particular you wanted to see me about?' she asked.

'No, nothing in particular. I just thought we might have a word.' He came to a stop just a couple of steps away. 'You know how I enjoy our little exchanges.' He smiled. 'So, tell me, how are things over at the centre? Are you still enjoying the job?'

'More than ever.'

'No regrets, then?'

'Not a single one. I can honestly say I've never enjoyed a job more.'

'You sound as though you mean that.'

'I wouldn't say it otherwise.'

As she looked at him, Carla was aware of the tension within her and of the unmistakably flinty edge to her voice. Last time, in a strange, perverse sort of way, she'd almost enjoyed their exchange on the stairs. It had been essentially light-hearted. Totally without hostility. But today there was anger and resentment in her heart. And, suddenly, she couldn't keep her feelings in any longer.

She narrowed her eyes at him and said in a cool tone, 'I suppose I really ought to congratulate you.'

'Congratulate me? On what?'

'On the coup you've pulled off. So, how does it feel to be the sole heir to Pentorra?' Jasper, she'd learned, had changed his will six months ago, so that now, instead of everything going jointly to Jedd and Nicholas, it would pass exclusively to Jedd.

Jedd ignored her question. 'You sound displeased with this development. I wonder why? What can it possibly matter to you?'

'It doesn't matter to me in the slightest. I just feel it's unfair.' Henrietta had told her about the tactics he'd used to ensure that Nicholas got written out of the will—a vicious campaign of character assassination that had finally worn down the already ailing old man. 'The whole thing sounds pretty tacky to me.'

'Does it, indeed?' He looked back at her, unblinking. 'Would I be right in assuming that you've been speaking to Henrietta?'

'You'd be absolutely right. She told me everything.'

'Oh, yes, I'll just bet she did. And you think it's unfair?'

'Totally.'

He smiled. 'Such loyalty to Nicholas. I have to say I'm deeply impressed.'

'Don't be. It's not loyalty. I just think he's had a bad deal.'

She did actually feel a bit sorry for Nicholas—who'd been so crushed by this development that he'd disappeared off to South America. But the core of Carla's feelings had nothing to do with Nicholas. She just felt angry with Jedd for what he'd done and the way he'd done it. She'd just said that it was tacky, but it was actually much worse than that.

She swung away now in disgust. 'Excuse me. I've got to catch the ferry.' And, grateful that he made no effort to stop her, she hurried off down the corridor to the stairs. Quite frankly, she couldn't bear to look into his face any more.

Yesterday, Henrietta had seen how angry her revelations had made Carla. She'd leaned across the table at The Griddle and told her, 'You know, you could help to put this mess right. You have influence with the old man. He likes you. He'd listen to you. Speak to him. See if you can help me change his mind. Between us maybe we could persuade him to put the will back to the way it was.'

'Oh, no. I couldn't do that.' In spite of her sympathies, Carla had been adamant. 'For a start, the whole thing's none of my business and, anyway, I wouldn't dream of putting pressure on Jasper. He's far too ill at the moment for anything like that. So I don't think you should either. It wouldn't be fair.'

Now, as she headed down the road to the quayside, Carla was remembering that conversation. Henrietta, she felt certain, would take her advice. In her anxiety about her brother, she obviously hadn't been thinking straight, for she'd surely never do anything to harm her uncle. Unlike Jedd, who'd behaved like an absolute ogre.

It was quite bad enough the way he'd stabbed Nicholas in the back, but the thing that had really shocked Carla to the core was his cynical treatment of the old man. How could he have been so utterly gross as to subject him to his money-grabbing campaign against his cousin?

At first, she really had found that hard to take in. 'Surely not?' she'd protested to Henrietta in disbelief. 'I've always had the impression that he genuinely cares about his uncle.'

But sorrowfully, Henrietta had shaken her head. 'It seems he cares rather more about the inheritance.'

Carla's steps clicked angrily along the pavement. To-day, when she'd finally looked into his eyes, she'd wondered if she might glimpse some previously missed sign of the monster that he clearly was. But, in fact, she'd seen nothing new, just the same Jedd as before—though a Jedd towards whom, she'd suddenly realised, her feelings had begun to soften fractionally almost without her being aware of it. Perhaps, she'd been starting to wonder, he wasn't so bad after all? Well, how about that for a bit of desperately poor judgement?

Never mind, she consoled herself. She'd caught herself in time. Her opinion of him was now right back where it had started.

So, why was she so angry? Why was she upset?

I'm upset, she told herself, because I hate people who're two-faced. And I'm angry because I was dumb enough to fall for his charade.

But there was more to it than that. For some inexplicable reason, she also felt cheated and bitterly let down. As though she'd reached out to take hold of something only to discover it wasn't there.

CHAPTER SEVEN

IT HAD started to rain just as Jedd was turning off the main road and by the time he reached the Starship Centre less than two minutes later it was absolutely bucketing down. Just like that, the heavens had opened. One minute, clear skies and brilliant sunshine, the next a positive deluge of water.

He smiled to himself as he drew in at the kerbside. Good old English weather. You could always rely on it to surprise you. And down in this remote south-western corner it tended to be more temperamental than an operatic diva. Not that he'd ever considered that to be a minus. It was just one of the endless list of things he loved about the place.

Switching off the engine, he reached up to check that the note for Annie was still there in his shirt pocket. He knew she was out, so he'd leave it with the secretary. If he could, he'd have waited, but he was in a bit of a rush.

It was at that precise moment, as he was about to push the door open and jump out, that the sound of laughing voices suddenly made him look up. Coming towards him was a group of half a dozen children all huddled together under one big striped umbrella that was being held aloft by a slim, dark-haired girl. They were all half soaked to the skin, especially the girl, but totally oblivious, having a whale of a time.

Intrigued, Jedd paused to watch, for none of the group

had noticed him, and it was only as they got closer that he recognised the girl. It was Carla. As he looked at her, he felt a strange jolt inside.

For, in an instant, he'd been swept back to that time on the boat. She'd looked like this then, drenched to the bone, her blonde hair so wet it had almost appeared brown. He sat staring at her, very still, a thousand thoughts going through his head.

They'd reached the gate of the centre now and she was pushing it open, ushering her high-spirited bunch of charges through it. Then they were hurrying up the path and disappearing through the front door.

Jedd remained sitting where he was, staring into space for a couple of minutes. That brief journey back in time had awakened so many emotions. Momentarily, he felt completely knocked out of kilter.

He gave himself a shake. You're in a hurry, remember, he told himself. And, pushing the door open, he jumped down onto the pavement and strode quickly through the gate towards the entrance.

There was no one in the secretary's office. Jedd hesitated and frowned, reluctant just to leave the envelope on the desk. I'll put it in Annie's cubby-hole outside the staffroom, he decided.

To get there he had to pass the classroom where Carla had taken her charges. He knew where they'd gone for he could hear the sound of children's voices. And, though he hadn't meant to, he paused outside the half-open door, careful to keep hidden as he peered curiously inside.

She was standing in the far corner wielding a large

blue towel, vigorously rubbing the hair of a helplessly giggling little girl.

'Stand still!' he heard her protest, though she was laughing herself. 'How can I do this properly if you keep wriggling about like a fish?'

Jedd watched, entranced. It was such a lovely scene, so utterly spontaneous, so full of warmth and good humour. And it was odd. He'd never seen her like this before.

At last, he stepped away and went to slip the note in Annie's cubby-hole. But as he hurried back outside, through the rain, to the car, he was aware of a new sense of purpose in his heart.

He'd often thought he'd quite enjoy a repeat of that episode on the boat. But suddenly his feelings had changed. Somehow he *had* to make it happen.

Carla was just about to climb aboard the ferry when she spotted him. It was exactly like that other time. He was marching along the quay, though she couldn't be certain whether he'd noticed her or not.

Don't kid yourself, a voice in her head advised her. He probably saw you before you saw him! Right this minute, he's on his way to pick up one of the private launches and, just like always, he'll be waiting at the top of the stairs when you arrive.

But he wasn't.

How strange. His spies were letting him down today!

'Carla!'

She was hurrying along the corridor to Jasper's room when someone suddenly stepped out of a doorway behind her, almost making her jump out of her skin. Her first thought was that it was Jedd, but, virtually simultaneously, she recognised the voice and realised it wasn't.

She whirled round. 'Henrietta! Good heavens, what a fright!'

'I'm sorry I startled you.' Henrietta gave her arm a squeeze. 'I was looking for you. I've something to tell you… Jedd's not here.'

'Are you sure?' Carla recounted how she'd seen him on the quay. 'Maybe he's on his way over right now.'

Henrietta shook her head. 'I spoke to Larry a couple of minutes ago and he told me that only one of the private launches is in use today…and that's over here. So, you see, he can't get back.'

Carla grimaced. 'I wouldn't count on it. If he finds out I'm here, quite frankly I wouldn't put it past him to swim!' Then her expression grew sober. There was an intense look in her friend's eyes. 'But why are you telling me all this? What's on your mind?'

'Carla, I need a favour… Remember what I asked you? If you'd have a word with Jasper? You know, about the inheritance…to try and get him to change his will back… Well, this is the perfect opportunity…Jedd's not here. You'll have the old man all to yourself.'

'But I told you I wouldn't do it. Henrietta, I wouldn't dream of it.' Carla frowned and shook her head. 'I'm sorry. But I explained why.'

'But you're our last hope. No one else can help. And the will's not fair. You said so yourself…'

'Henrietta, there's no way—'

'Carla, I'm desperate.' She came closer, her grip

around Carla's arm tightening. 'Look, I promise you that Nicholas and I would make it worth your while.'

'*What?*' Carla was aghast. 'I don't believe you just said that!' Angrily, she pulled her arm free. 'I'm going to see your uncle now. I don't think we should talk about this any more.' And she whirled round and went stalking off down the corridor.

The next thirty-five minutes or so with Jasper calmed her down. He was in remarkably high spirits and looking really good today—positively pink-cheeked, a wicked sparkle in his eyes as he sat straight-backed against the linen pillows.

They chatted away as usual about all sorts of things—music, the weather, *Baywatch*, food… Conversation was never a problem between her and Jasper. Then he asked her about the children and she told him a bit of what they'd been up to and just happened to touch on the subject of Freddie and his nightmares, for he'd had another one just the other night.

'Poor little devil.' The old man's face filled with compassion. 'It's such a mercy that you can be there for him.'

Carla sighed. 'I know, but I won't be around for long. It makes me feel so sad. Heaven knows what'll become of him. He's on his own, you see. No parents. No family. I know they do their best for him at the children's home where he lives, but—' She broke off, swallowed hard and shook her head. 'I just wish I could wrap him up and take him home with me.'

It was only after she'd left Jasper and was making her way downstairs that her thoughts went back to her earlier encounter with Henrietta. That had definitely been a bit off. But she no longer felt angry. Her chat with Jasper had mellowed her mood. The poor girl must have had some kind of mental seizure, she decided. And, since she hated to part on a disagreeable note, it might be a good idea to try and find her and have a word. Though only a very quick one, for she was running a bit late.

She decided to try the drawing room first, but there was nobody there. She sighed. What now? She started to turn away…only to suffer her second near heart attack of the afternoon as she found herself walking slap-bang into Jedd.

'Are you looking for Henrietta again? Well, I'm afraid she's not here. It's the familiar old story. She saw I was back and instantly fled.'

Carla was still catching her breath. 'Must you keep creeping up on me all the time?' She flared an angry look at him and took a hurried step back. For far worse than the fright he'd given her had been the actual physical collision. She could still feel the hard heat of him burning into her flesh.

'I didn't mean to give you a fright. I didn't even know you were there. I thought you were probably still upstairs with the old man.'

What? Had she heard right? He'd known she was here, yet he hadn't come rushing upstairs to keep an eye on her?

She peered at him curiously. 'How long have you been back?'

'Half an hour or so.'

This was just too bizarre. Not the fact that he'd got back when there were supposedly no boats—the explanation for that was probably that he'd got a lift from someone. She stared at him. 'And you left me alone with your uncle?' *That* was the thing that just didn't make sense! 'How come? Maybe you thought it was too late to bother, that I'd already persuaded him to part with the family silver?'

'Maybe I did…though I could easily have come back earlier. You see, I saw you get on the ferry…and there was room. I could have joined you.'

Carla was speechless for a moment. 'So, why on earth didn't you?'

'I had an appointment in town that I didn't want to miss. So I decided to take a risk and let you off the leash this once.'

'Oh, did you?' She felt like punching his condescending nose. Off the leash, indeed! What was she? His wretched dog? 'Well, maybe that was just a bit rash of you,' she challenged. 'Who knows what I might have got up to in your absence?'

He seemed peculiarly unconcerned. 'So, what did you get up to? How many tens of thousands did you manage to get your hands on?'

'None, as a matter of fact.'

'And what about the family silver?'

'Not even a teaspoon.'

'Oh, dear. You obviously haven't been trying.'

Carla tilted her head at him. 'Maybe I haven't quite got into my stride yet. Maybe I like to work up to things slowly. You know, prepare the ground first. Work out a plan.'

'So perhaps I'd be wise not to let you off the leash too often?'

As he smiled, Carla felt herself smile back in response, which really didn't feel like what she ought to be doing. Wasn't she supposed to be mad at him…to have written him off? Hadn't she decided he was nothing but a ghastly, grasping monster?

To be perfectly honest, she'd been battling with that idea pretty well ceaselessly since their last meeting. She kept telling herself it was the plain, simple truth, yet there was something about Henrietta's story that bothered her. So far, she'd been unable to put her finger on what it was, but a tiny doubt continued to niggle at the back of her mind.

And it was all highly confusing. Especially at this moment, as she stood there smiling at him, feeling the warmth that flowed between them, and not knowing what to think at all.

For a moment or two neither of them spoke, just continued to watch one another in silence. Then suddenly Jedd said, 'How come you ever gave up teaching?' He made it sound as thought it was something to regret.

Carla studied him curiously. 'This is a bit of a turn-around! I thought what you found strange was that I ever took it up in the first place! Didn't you once say that you thought PR was more my sort of thing?'

'You're right. I did. But I think I may have been mistaken. From what I've seen, I suspect you're probably a born teacher.'

Carla blinked at him. 'I'm afraid you're going to have to explain that.'

'I saw you the other day. You didn't see me. I came to the centre to hand in a letter and I saw you coming back in the rain with the children. I'm afraid I hung around and watched you for a bit. And I saw what you're like with them. You clearly have a special gift.'

'Well, I don't know about that.' She fought back a blush. 'I love working with them, that's all, and maybe it shows.'

'Oh, it definitely shows.' He smiled a small smile. 'Were you always a teacher, then, before you switched to PR?'

'Always. It was the only thing I ever wanted to be. From when I was about ten, I think—or maybe even younger. I used to take classes with my dolls and the family cat.'

She stopped, in spite of an urge to go on and tell him more. Surely he couldn't really be interested in all this?

But it seemed that he was. 'Are there other teachers in your family?'

'No. Not a single one. I sprang out of nowhere. But I got loads of encouragement. Right from when I was small.'

'So, why on earth did you give it up? Did you just get tired, feel like a change?'

'No.' Carla hesitated. 'It wasn't like that.' All at once, she was aware of a conflict inside her.

'Did you lose your job?'

She shook her head. It was weird. She wanted to tell him. But this was Jedd, remember? And since when did she confide in Jedd? 'No,' she said. 'It wasn't that either.'

'So, what was the reason?' He was leaning towards her, peering at her as though he'd like to see inside her head.

'Something personal. A family matter.' Carla detached her gaze from his, aware of a sudden anxious tension inside her. All of a sudden, she felt threatened. He was getting too close.

She took a step back. 'I have to go now. The ferry…' She glanced at her watch and instantly froze. 'Oh, no! Look at the time! I'll never catch it now!'

Jedd was checking his own watch. 'You're right. Let's get moving.' He turned and began to head swiftly across the hall. 'I'll give you a lift. It's my fault for holding you up.'

Carla followed him with her eyes, but remained standing where she was. This wasn't what she wanted. What she wanted was to escape from him. The very last thing she fancied right now was climbing into his car with him and going for a cosy little drive.

'What's wrong? What are you waiting for?' He paused in the doorway and frowned at her. 'We've only got a couple of minutes.'

Carla still didn't move. Then she gave herself a shake. What choice did she have? 'Okay,' she said. 'I'm coming.'

Throughout the mercifully brief journey down to the harbour, Carla was careful not to glance at him even once. Quite frankly, she didn't dare. Something very odd was happening to her and sitting there beside him in that small enclosed space was having the most alarming effect on her equilibrium. She could feel his physical nearness like a warm weight against her. Every time he changed gear, her heart rate broke into a gallop.

He made no attempt at conversation, for which she was profoundly glad, for she doubted her ability to put two words sensibly together. But there was nothing remotely soothing about the silence between them. It was as taut as a piece of elastic stretched to its limits.

At last, they were down on the quay, drawing up alongside the ferry, which Carla was relieved to see was still loading passengers. She half turned to look at Jedd as she reached for the door handle, about to thank him for the lift before leaping out and fleeing. But something made her pause, something in his expression as he swivelled round to face her and asked yet another unexpected question.

'Where did you get the name Carla from? It's not one you come across often.'

'It was my grandmother's name.' She watched him curiously as she answered. 'You see, my mother was Italian. From Arezzo, a town near Florence.'

'Ah.' He smiled at her. 'You don't look Italian.'

'No, I suppose not. I don't exactly fit the stereotype. But not all Italians have dark hair and brown eyes, you know. In fact, my mother had virtually the same colouring as me.'

She saw him frown and instantly guessed why. Somehow, by her tone or a fleeting shadow across her eyes, she must surely have betrayed the catch of pain in her heart as she'd made that brief reference to her beloved dead mother. She knew it still happened, though it was only very rarely that anyone was sensitive enough to actually pick it up. The last person she'd ever have expected to do so was Jedd.

Abruptly, she glanced away. 'Thanks for the lift,' she told him. Then she was snatching the door open and jumping down from the car.

She didn't turn to look back until she was safely on

board the ferry, though somehow, instinctively, she knew he was still there. It was only as the pilot's mate began to cast off that she saw the Land Rover do a U-turn and head back along the quay.

Carla watched it till it disappeared, aware that her heart was pumping anxiously, the way it did when you missed your footing hurrying down a flight of steps. And, out of nowhere, something suddenly seemed to clarify inside her brain.

That niggling little doubt that had been bothering her for days…all at once she knew exactly what it was. She hadn't wanted to think this, but it was a question she had to ask. Was it possible that Henrietta's story about Jedd might not be true?

Carla's next encounter with Jedd came a couple of days later when she arrived at the castle to pay Jasper another visit. He was driving out through the gates just as she was walking in.

She half expected that he'd instantly change direction and follow her back inside again. But, instead, he pulled up and leaned through the driver's window.

'He's not so good today. He had a bit of a bad night. So it's best if you keep it brief. He tires easily on days like this.'

Then, before she could open her mouth, with a quick wave he was driving off.

Carla watched him disappear. Curiouser and curiouser. Did this mean he had another appointment he didn't want to miss or had he decided to let her off the leash permanently?

Don't start getting too optimistic, she told herself. More than likely, it's just the former.

He'd been right about his uncle. Jasper didn't look good today, though it was obvious that he was pleased to see her.

'Sit down and chat to me,' he told her, patting the bedspread. 'Though I'm afraid you'll have to do most of the talking. I'll just lie here and do the listening.'

And that was exactly what happened, though he stirred himself at one point and demanded to know, 'How's young Freddie doing?'

Carla smiled at him. 'Like you, he has good days and bad days. Unfortunately, the nightmares are still a problem. He had another one last night, though not as bad as before. I had to stay with him for well over an hour.'

'You want to watch it, young lady, or you'll wear yourself out!'

'Oh, don't worry about me. I'll manage all right.' Carla patted his hand as he frowned with concern. 'I just wish I could find a way to stop the nightmares. He's such a nice kid, really, when you get to know him.' She smiled as she thought of the bright little face beneath the thatch of unruly red hair, and the eyes that could be so fierce and yet so vulnerable at the same time. 'I guess he just needs someone to love him.'

As she paused, she was aware that the old man was watching her. He shook his head and smiled. 'You're such a nice girl, Carla. As I'm always saying to Jedd, if I was forty years younger I think I'd probably ask you to marry me.'

Carla smiled to herself as she thought about that on the way home. It had been a sweet thing to say, but she couldn't help wondering how Jedd responded when his uncle said such things. Jasper hadn't told her that!

Knowing Jedd, he probably didn't respond at all, just kept his opinions to himself. But what were those opinions? Had they mellowed at all? She remembered that last conversation they'd had. Had the warmth she'd felt between them been real or had she imagined it? Over the past couple of days, she'd thought about that a lot.

Too much, she chastised herself. Far too much. And she'd also become just a little too obsessed with trying to sort out her feelings for him.

These had definitely changed. She liked him more and more. There were so many nice sides to him that she hadn't known before. And another crucial point... After a great deal of thought, she'd become totally, utterly and unshakeably convinced that what Henrietta had told her about him couldn't possibly be true.

Carla had agonised about that. Why would Henrietta lie? The only reason she could think of was to blacken Jedd's name and try to get Carla on her side. But she felt ashamed of even thinking such a horrible thing about her friend. Henrietta had always been protective of her brother, but she just wasn't the type to go in for such horrible, vindictive slander.

It was all very weird. Maybe there'd been some kind of misunderstanding? But one thing was certain. There was no way in the world that Jedd would ever do anything that might harm the old man—like deliberately wear him down, as Henrietta had claimed, with a campaign of slanders and lies against his cousin. Whatever else he might be capable of, Carla was quite certain that he'd never put his uncle's health at risk.

She'd thought about it endlessly, wondering if maybe she was just telling herself this because she didn't want to believe that he could do such a thing. But it had nothing to do with her own feelings, she'd finally decided. Jedd truly loved his uncle and that was all there was to it. If it was true that he was the one who'd persuaded his uncle to change his will, it definitely hadn't happened the way Henrietta had described.

Still, none of this was any excuse for thinking about him all the time! She stopped herself in mid-thought. Here she was doing it again! It really was getting to be a bit of a habit. And he wasn't that important to her, nor ever would be, she reminded herself sharply. Had she forgotten he was Annie's secret lover?

For that was definitely the case, though Annie was still playing her little game, trying to pretend it wasn't Jedd on the phone when Carla knew perfectly well that it was, then sneaking off for clandestine little meetings at the Partridge Inn. So, Carla's feelings for him, when it came down to it, were neither here nor there. The plain fact was that he was strictly out of bounds.

That thought did the trick. She switched her mind to other things, like the painting class she'd be taking later this afternoon and for which she'd just thought of the perfect theme.

'Paint me a picture,' she'd invite her charges, 'of the Invisible Man!'

'Jedd came up with a really nice idea last night. He suggested that we teachers take it in turn to accompany a group of the older children to the island—and stay there for two or three days. The kids could visit the bird sanctuary, go swimming and stuff like that.'

Carla looked at Annie as the two of them sat in her office chatting over a mug of coffee. 'Sounds interesting,' she replied, 'but would we actually need to stay over?' That bit sounded a bit too cosy for comfort! 'I mean, couldn't we just organise a couple of day trips or something?'

'That's what I said, too, but Jedd insisted. And I suppose he's right. There's loads of room at the castle and we wouldn't have to waste time going backwards and forwards.'

Damn Jedd and his logic. 'Yes, I suppose so.'

'I suggested that you might like to take the first group—a bunch of the older boys—at the beginning of next week.' Annie smiled brightly across at her. 'How does that sound?'

Carla swallowed and did her best to smile brightly back. 'Great,' she said. 'It sounds absolutely fine.'

Leaning back in her chair, Carla glanced down with a smile at the semicircle of rapt-faced, pyjama-clad little boys seated cross-legged on the floor at her feet.

'That's all for tonight,' she said, closing the book she'd been reading them. 'You'll have to wait till tomorrow night to find out what happens next.'

There was a collective groan of protest.

'Please… Just one more page…'

'Go on, Miss Roberts…'

'Another five minutes…'

But she refused to be moved. Good-naturedly, she shook her head. 'Not even half a minute. It's time you were all in bed.' For she could see that, in spite of these attempts to win her round, the only thing keeping her audience awake was determination. Which was scarcely surprising. It had been a pretty exhausting day.

They'd arrived on the island for their three-day stay shortly after nine o'clock this morning and in the intervening thirteen hours they'd scarcely stopped for breath.

A game of five-a-side football, a swim in the bay in the late afternoon and a search in the rock pools for crabs before the tide came in. Oh, yes, and a hilarious game of hide-and-seek in which Jimmy had rather given his position away by falling in a giggling heap from an apple tree—fortunately without damage either to the tree or himself.

And now, in the ten beds that were arranged round the room, were ten sleepy but perfectly contented little faces. One by one, Carla went round to tuck them in and kiss them goodnight.

'See you in the morning,' she whispered as she switched off the light after casting a special quick glance across at Freddie. Then she smiled to herself. Naturally, there'd been no response. Half of them, including Freddie, were already fast asleep!

She slipped through the door and pulled it closed without a sound—then abruptly spun round, aware of a pair of eyes on her.

'I hope I didn't startle you.' Jedd was standing just across the corridor. 'It seems to be rather an unfortunate habit of mine.'

There was no arguing with that! 'Yes, it is,' she agreed, though it wasn't the sudden fright that was making her heart race.

He was dressed in a pair of putty-coloured chinos and a plain white shirt. The dark hair was pushed away from the tanned, bony face and was damp, as though he'd recently had a shower. Carla looked at him and was aware of desire tightening inside her. The wet hair. The storm. The boat. The famous kiss.

'So, are you finished at last?' He smiled as he looked at her. 'It's been quite a day. Do you always work this hard?'

'It's not always quite so strenuous, but this is generally when I knock off. Naturally, I have to see the kids to bed.'

'So, you *are* finished. That's good...because the reason I came to find you was to ask if you'd like to join me downstairs for a drink.'

Oh, no. Definitely not. She had to find a way out of this.

'I'm sorry, but I can't. I'm just off to look in on Jasper.' It was actually the truth. She'd been thinking that she might. 'Sorry,' she said again, sighing inwardly, feeling safe.

But the feeling was short-lived.

'He's already asleep. I went to see him just a couple of minutes ago.' Jedd smiled. 'Come on. Let's go and have that drink and you can put your feet up for half an hour.'

There was nothing Carla felt like more than relaxing for a while. But definitely not with Jedd. That would not be a good idea. She searched her brain for some excuse, but came up with zero. 'I don't really feel like a drink,' she said, shaking her head.

'Nonsense. Of course you do.' He waved aside her

protest. 'Come on. I insist.' And he reached out his hand and, before she could stop him, took hold of her arm.

Carla froze, fighting the rush of sensation that swept through her. She mustn't let him insist. That could prove fatal. Snatching a huge breath, she tensed herself to pull free.

But, just at the crucial moment, he looked into her face and smiled, and next thing she knew she was following him down the corridor, without a single word of protest, like a lamb to the slaughter.

CHAPTER EIGHT

A COUPLE of minutes later, Carla was out on the terrace with a large glass of five-star brandy in her hand.

It was a beautiful night, the air sweet and balmy, the sky studded with starlight, the moon big and bright, and part of her longed just to relax and enjoy it. Another part, however, with a much louder voice, was warning her that, simply by being here, she was playing with fire. Which was why she was sitting very upright in her chair looking like a rather nervous sparrow poised for flight.

The only thing to do was keep this very brief. She took a swig of her drink, very nearly choked and had to fight to catch her breath. Lesson one. Brandy ought to be sipped slowly, not gulped!

Jedd, totally at ease, sat watching her across the table.

'So,' he said, 'you're taking the kids to the sanctuary tomorrow? I'd have come with you, but unfortunately I've got an appointment in town.'

Once, Carla would have found it hard to believe that he'd be interested in visiting a bird sanctuary with a bunch of kids. But not any more. Especially after today, for he'd impressed her with the way he'd been so good with the boys, chatting to them and introducing them to Buster, his black Labrador, who'd been a huge hit, particularly with Freddie. Later, he'd even offered to referee their football game and had told them all the best rock pools for finding crabs.

'But Larry's going with you, so you'll be in good hands,' he continued. 'He'll be taking you by the over-land route in the minibus. I think that's the best way.' He cast her a quick smile, deliberately holding her eyes as he added, 'It might be asking for trouble to go by the sea route. You never know what nasty little surprises the weather might pull.'

Very funny. Carla pulled a face. The sea route to the sanctuary was more or less the same one that she'd taken to get to Gull Point a couple of years ago—you then climbed up the cliffs where a pathway had been cut.

'Indeed,' she agreed briefly, not wishing to dwell on the subject. There was no need to bring that infamous storm into the conversation!

Jedd continued to smile as he took a sip of his brandy, but at least he had the grace to change the subject. 'I get the impression the kids are really looking forward to the trip.'

'They are. They're really excited.' Carla felt herself relax a bit. 'We spent a couple of hours with Annie's nature book last night, studying all the different birds we're hoping to see.'

'They'll probably spot quite a few. Some redwings for sure. There are lots of them about this year.'

Carla watched him, aware again of that sense of har-mony between them. How strange, she reflected. It was almost getting to be a habit. Something fundamental had altered.

Today, after the boys had gone off to the stables for their riding lesson, Carla had dropped by to spend half an hour with Jasper—Annie had insisted that the chil-dren's riding time be her free time!—and, again, Jedd hadn't bothered to come and sit in with her, though she knew he'd seen her go upstairs. And, whenever their paths crossed, he was friendly and charming, in a perfectly natural and unforced sort of way. At times it was hard to believe things hadn't always been this way.

He was watching her over his glass. 'You're really fond of these kids, aren't you? I came along near the end of that bedtime story you were reading and it was perfectly obvious the way you feel about them.'

Carla nodded. 'Yes, I am enormously fond of them,' she agreed.

He smiled. 'You seem to have a bit of a soft spot for that little redhead. Not,' he added quickly at her instant look of guilt, 'that I think either he or any of the other kids are aware of it. But there's definitely a special tenderness in your eyes when you look at him.'

'Really?' She sighed. 'Sometimes you can't help it. You try your best to care equally for all of them, but now and then there's one who just stirs something in you.'

'And what does Freddie stir in you?'

'I don't know.' She glanced away and stared down for a moment at the terracotta tiles. But she could feel that he was still watching her, waiting for her to continue. She looked up at him and shrugged. 'Maybe,' she added evasively, 'there's something in him that I recognise.'

'What, for example?'

Again, she dropped her eyes. 'I don't know,' she insisted, wishing he would stop.

He allowed a moment to pass. Then he said, his tone soft, 'My guess is it's something to do with your mother.

Your fair-haired Italian mother whom you obviously
adored.' He paused. 'Has Freddie lost his mother, too?'

Carla's eyes jerked up again. She felt a mix of emotions. Surprise at the insight. Resentment at the intrusion.
She was about to say, None of that's any of your business! but at the look on his face the words died in her
throat.

She could see he understood. Her pain. Her sense of
loss. The terrible grief that sometimes still tore at her.
He'd been down that road himself. He'd suffered these
things too.

He was leaning towards her. 'I'm right, am I not?'

Carla nodded. 'Yes, you are. Freddie's mother died
six months ago. And the poor little soul doesn't even
have a father.'

'Again like you?'

'My father died when I was ten.' She straightened and
shook off the momentary darkness that had touched her
soul. 'But at least I had my mother until two and a half
years ago. And all my aunts and uncles, both here and
in Italy. Poor little Freddie's got nobody at all.'

There was another short silence. She looked at Jedd
and he looked back at her. Then he said, 'Was it because
of your mother's death that you gave up teaching?'

'Yes.' How had he guessed that? But she didn't mind
that he had. Eyes unseeing, she stared into her lap as she
continued. 'She was ill for a long time. Cancer. It was
terrible. And there was no way I could leave her to die
on her own. So I gave up my job and went back to
Walthamstow to nurse her. She'd always looked after
me. It was the least I could do.

'And afterwards...' She paused and closed her eyes

with a sigh. This was the bit he'd never make any sense of. Sometimes she had trouble understanding it herself. She shook her head. 'It was as though my whole world had caved in. Everything I'd ever cared about suddenly seemed meaningless. I did nothing for a couple of months. I was too numb. Barely functioning. And I just couldn't face the thought of going back to teaching. Then a friend told me about this PR job that was going. She knew the director. She said she'd fix up an interview.'

Carla took a deep breath and focused squarely on his face. 'It was so totally different from anything I'd ever done. Taking that job was almost like becoming another person. Stepping out of my old life, away from the grief and pain. I think I believed if I could become someone else for a while I might stand a better chance of surviving.'

'And that was when you met Nicholas?'

'Yes, shortly after that. He was part of my new disguise. What I needed at the time. But of course, in the long term, there was no way it could work—'

She broke off, not wanting to sound critical of Nicholas. They'd been too different, that was all. They hadn't cared about the same things. Gradually, she'd realised their relationship was a mistake.

A wry smile touched her lips. 'I found out it's pointless to run away from yourself. So, after a while, I decided to come back.'

Jedd said nothing for a moment, then he smiled a warm smile. 'I'd say you definitely did the right thing.'

Carla looked at him, feeling a strange, quiet bond of understanding. Most times, when she tried to explain that mixed-up period of her life, she could tell that the other person didn't really grasp what it had been about. But she sensed that Jedd did and she liked the way that felt.

Don't like it too much! The warning rang in her head. For suddenly she was aware that there was something going on between them.

He was watching her with a look so hungry and intense that it almost felt as though it might swallow her up, and she was sitting there glowing like a hundred-watt light bulb that somebody had just switched on. This is dangerous, she told herself. It's time you got out of here.

'So, after you went back to yourself…was that when you cut your hair?'

As he spoke, Jedd leaned a little closer towards her, putting down his glass, as though to leave his hands free. He's about to do something, Carla thought, a helpless panic driving through her. He's going to touch me. I just know it. And the awful thing is I want him to.

'Yes,' she said as he reached out one hand to stroke her cheek.

Carla was holding her breath, her heart racing inside her, though all she was aware of was the heat of his fingers as he lazily tucked a strand of her hair behind her ear.

'Definitely a good move.' He smiled a slow, lingering smile that made it hard for her to focus on his eyes. Involuntarily, her gaze dropped down to his lips.

She could imagine them on her own. Cool and hard and sensuous. And suddenly, more than anything, she longed to close her eyes and relive the excitement of when they'd kissed on the boat.

Oh, no! She had to stop this! She snatched a quick breath and pulled herself up against the back of her seat.

'I think I ought to go now.' She pushed back her chair. 'It's been a long day and I've got an early start tomorrow.' Before she'd finished the sentence, she was on her feet and stepping away.

'But you haven't finished your drink. Surely there's no need to go rushing off?'

Oh, but there was. 'I really think I ought to go. Bed's what I need now.' She instantly wished she hadn't said that. 'I mean sleep,' she amended quickly, only making matters worse. 'I'm whacked.' She smiled lamely. 'I'd better say goodnight.'

'I'll see you to your room.'

'No. Please. There's no need.' She waved a protesting hand at him as he seemed about to stand up. 'Just stay where you are.' She began to back away. 'Goodnight and thanks for the brandy.' And she almost ran out the door.

Carla cursed herself all the way back to her room. What an idiot she must have looked. Like some silly, startled virgin. What in heaven's name was the matter with her? What had happened to her cool?

Actually, she knew the answer to that one all too well. It had been blown into a million stupefied fragments the instant his fingers had made contact with her skin. It was perfectly pathetic, but that really was the truth.

She closed the bedroom door, but didn't switch the light on, then crossed to the window and drew one curtain back a little. It was just as she'd thought. Her window overlooked the terrace. She stiffened, her stomach twisting, as she suddenly caught sight of him.

He was standing at the edge of the terrace, his back towards her, gazing out over the castle grounds. She saw him raise his glass and drink, saw a flash of moonlight in his hair, then he was heading for the steps that led down into the garden. Breathing slowly, Carla stood very still and watched.

At the top of the steps, he paused and suddenly turned round, and it seemed to Carla that he was looking straight at her.

He couldn't possibly have seen her, of course, but with a little gasp she drew back, letting the curtain fall shut again, her heart beating fast.

Jedd drained his glass, set it down on the garden wall and, slipping his hands into his trouser pockets, continued down the steps to the stone flagged path.

He often came to walk in the floodlit garden at night. After a hard day running around the estate in the car or, like today, when he'd been stuck for hours behind his desk—the part of his job he definitely enjoyed least!—he found it a perfect way to unwind. He loved the silence, the soft evening scents, knowing that no one was there but him. He often used this time to plan his schedule for the next day.

Tonight, however, his mind wasn't on work. He was thinking about what had just passed between him and Carla...and about what might have developed if she hadn't gone running off like that! He smiled wryly to himself. A large part of his time these days was taken up with engaging in such thoughts about Carla. For this attraction he felt to her just got stronger and stronger. She was starting to turn into a dangerous obsession.

He must have wandered round the garden for a good forty minutes and when he got back to the terrace he wasn't surprised to see that Carla's bedroom window was in darkness. Almost certainly, she was fast asleep by now. Good, he thought. She'd been looking a little tired.

Back inside the house, he made his way upstairs, careful not to make any noise. It was a pity he was going to be so tied up tomorrow that he wouldn't be able to go on the trip to see the birds. It would've been nice to spend a day out with her—even though, needless to say, with all the kids there, any thoughts of romance would have been strictly out of bounds!

At that moment, just as he reached the top of the stairs, he heard cries coming from the direction of the corridor where the boys slept. Next instant, there was the sound of a door bursting open, then a figure went racing across the end of the corridor, hair flying, pulling on her dressing gown as she went. As she disappeared from view, he heard another door open. An instant later, the crying stopped.

Jedd stopped in his tracks. What the devil was going on? Wasn't Carla supposed to be fast asleep in bed?

Next morning, as she was in the kitchen preparing breakfast for the boys—with the help of Mrs Pickles, the housekeeper, and Lucy, the maid—Carla received a most peculiar phone call from Annie.

'Look, I can't stop to talk…we've got a bit of a crisis on here…but I want you to take the day off today, Carla. In fact, I insist. Bertha's coming over to stand in for you. She's actually on her way. She'll be there in about half an hour.

'Listen, I'm sorry but I've got to go,' she added quickly before Carla could answer. An instant later, the phone went dead.

So, what was that all about? Why was she supposed to take the day off? Maybe Bertha—a summer recruit like herself—would be able to shed some light when she arrived?

But when, thirty-five minutes later, Bertha stepped from the taxi that Carla had sent to pick her up from the ferry all she could do was shake her head.

'I haven't a clue,' she confessed. 'I didn't speak to Annie. She was up to her eyes with plumbers and a burst pipe. It was the secretary who told me I had to come straight over and relieve you.'

She shrugged good-naturedly, glanced around her and grinned. 'Well, I'm not complaining. What a fabulous place!'

Carla was baffled. So, what was she supposed to do? Sit around for the rest of the day and count her toes?

'Listen,' she told Bertha, 'as long as you've no objections, I'd like to come along anyway with you and the boys to the sanctuary. Naturally, you're in charge. I'll just take a back seat. But I've actually rather been looking forward to the trip.'

Besides, it would be nice to spend the day with Bertha. A middle-aged divorcee with a grown-up family, she was excellent company and she and Carla got on well.

Bertha didn't mind at all. 'That's fine by me,' she said.

There was another reason why Carla wanted to go on the trip—or, rather, why she was less than keen to remain at the castle. If she stayed, there was a risk she might bump into Jedd and that would definitely not be a good idea. Last night had been a very clear warning indeed that things were in danger of getting too chummy between them. It would be wise if, from now on, she were to keep out of his way.

Alas, she didn't entirely manage to do that. He appeared just as she and Bertha and the children were getting ready to set off in the minibus with Larry.

They were all gathered out in the driveway when the Land Rover came round the corner. Carla braced herself as Jedd jumped out and started to come towards them, with Buster trotting at his heels. Please don't let him have changed his mind about coming, she prayed silently.

'I see you're all set to go.' Jedd glanced round at the children. 'I'll expect to hear all about it when you get back.' As he spoke, he ruffled Johnny's spiky blond hair. 'You must give me a complete run-down of all the birds you manage to see.'

Good. He wasn't coming. Carla sighed with relief. And, even better, he'd barely even glanced at her. He must have rethought last night and realised it had been a mistake.

He was turning to Bertha. 'You must be Mrs Austen?' As they shook hands, Carla decided Mrs Pickles must have told him. 'Welcome to the island,' he told her. Then he looked round at the boys again. 'Okay, you'd better get going. I hope you all have a fabulous time.'

'Can Buster come with us?' Suddenly Freddie piped

up. He looked adoringly at the big, good-natured dog. 'I'm sure he'd enjoy it,' he added, glancing up at Jedd.

'Yes, let him come!' As Jedd hesitated for a moment, another couple of wheedling voices chipped in.

Jedd smile. 'I don't see why not. He can stay in the bus while you're watching the birds. And I'm sure he'd enjoy going for a walk with you all afterwards.'

'But hang on…' At the instant whoops of approval, he raised his hand. 'I'm not the one in charge here. It's up to Miss Roberts and Mrs Austen to decide.' With a smile, he turned at last to look at Carla.

Carla hated the way her heart leapt as she met the grey gaze. She stifled the feeling instantly and glanced round at the boys, who were now directing all their pleas at her.

'Go on, Miss Roberts!'

'Say yes!'

'Please let him come!'

Carla smiled. 'Well, it's perfectly fine by me, but I'm afraid the last word has to be with Mrs Austen. She's actually the one in charge today.'

Bertha laughed as all eyes swivelled anxiously to her. 'Of course he can come with us,' she declared—though no one actually heard the last part of the sentence which was totally drowned in a chorus of cheers.

'Larry can take charge of him.' Jedd patted the dog's black head. 'Not that he'll be any trouble. He doesn't need looking after.' Then, making the children laugh, he added with a wink, 'He knows every inch of the island like the back of his paw.'

Five minutes later, the boys were all aboard, buckled into their seats and ready to go.

Carla climbed up beside Bertha as Jedd bade them goodbye. 'Have a good trip,' he called—though to the children, not to her. Then the bus was setting off and Jedd was heading back to the Land Rover.

Carla watched him through the wing mirror, pretending she really wasn't, and wondered if he'd be going to see Annie today.

Four bullfinches, three redwings, two mistle thrushes and a rook—and that was all within the first half-hour. The trip to the sanctuary was a huge success.

The boys crouched in their wooden hides, field glasses pressed against their noses, as still as statues, scarcely breathing, totally enthralled by this new adventure. The only sound to break the silence was the occasional hushed cry of wonder as some new bird suddenly made its appearance through the trees.

Carla spent most of her time watching the boys rather than the birds, deeply moved by the expressions on their faces. Coming here had been an inspired idea. It was an experience that none of them would ever forget.

Afterwards, they drove to a quiet spot for a picnic lunch, then sat around for a while just talking about what they'd seen. It was a beautiful day. Scarcely a cloud in the sky. It seemed to Carla that the whole thing simply couldn't have been more perfect.

'How about a walk now to help work off that lunch?' For every single scrap of Mrs Pickles' generous hamper—apart from the chicken bones and the plastic wrappers—had been consumed to the very last crumb! As she and Bertha started to clear up, Carla looked round at the eager faces. 'Just give us a hand with this lot, then we can go.'

Larry led the way as, ten minutes later they set off, following the track that wound round by the cliffs. Carla and Bertha took up the rearguard, keeping an eye on the slower children, while some of the other boys, including Freddie—who was looking not at all like his usual withdrawn self—went bounding ahead with Buster.

'Stay together!' Carla called after them. 'And don't let Larry out of your sight.' She and Bertha were taking turns to shout out instructions and were doing head counts just about every five seconds!

It was about thirty minutes into their walk that it suddenly happened. As the two women came round a narrow bend, Freddie came running towards them.

'It's Buster. He's gone.' The poor child was close to tears. 'He saw a rabbit and went chasing after it. He's going to get lost.'

'No, he won't.' Carla remembered what Jedd had said earlier. 'Just give him a couple of minutes. You'll see, he'll soon come back.'

But Freddie wasn't listening. He swung away. 'I'm going after him!' And before she could stop him he was haring off between the trees.

'Freddie! Come back! Freddie! Freddie!' Carla rushed to the edge of the path and called after him. But she knew it was pointless. She'd seen the look in his eyes. He believed his beloved Buster was in danger.

There was only one thing to do. She turned quickly to Bertha. 'I'm going after him,' she declared. 'Tell Larry what's happened.'

Then, without another word, she plunged into the trees.

CHAPTER NINE

'FREDDIE! Where are you? Freddie, come back!'

Once out of the trees, the path broke up into several trails, all of them leading down towards the cliffs. Carla picked one at random, for there was no sign of either boy or dog, then, off to her right, she caught a sudden flash of red hair.

Damn! She'd gone the wrong way. She doubled back at once. 'Freddie, come back! Freddie! Freddie!' But, the very next instant, he'd disappeared again.

She was getting close to the cliff edge now. She could hear the sound of the sea. Panting for breath, she stopped and peered round.

And there he was, right at the edge. She headed towards him, though she didn't bother to shout this time, for there was absolutely no chance he'd hear. For one thing, the wind was blowing the wrong way. But then, all of a sudden, there was no sign of him any more.

Still, there was only one way he could have gone. She started to plunge down the jagged precipice, slipping and skidding as small stones gave way beneath her feet. Then, off in the distance she caught another glimpse of red—though how he'd managed to get over there heaven alone knew! He'd ended up on a ledge at the other side of a rocky maze. The child must be some kind of mountain goat!

Picking her way carefully, Carla headed towards him, at times down on all fours, at others sliding on her bot-

128

tom. She was almost there when, in her anxiety, she stumbled awkwardly and fell, but, ignoring the wrench in her ankle, she gritted her teeth and carried on. There were only a few metres to go now. Just a small outcrop to get past. As she rounded it, she felt a quick, warm squeeze of anticipation. 'Freddie!' she called out. 'Freddie, I'm here!'

Then she froze. Oh, no! It wasn't Freddie at all. Waving in the wind, seeming to mock her, was a thick, bushy clump of orange-red flowers.

For a moment, Carla just crouched there, her heart pounding, catching her breath. Where had he gone? She was losing precious time. She'd have to go back and try another route.

But, as she turned, she saw instantly that taking the same way back was out of the question. Scrambling down had been hard enough; trying to do the reverse would be impossible.

In despair, she looked round. There was only one solution. If she carried on down, maybe she could find an easier way to get back up.

Almost weeping with frustration, she continued her descent. By the time she finally reached him, who knew what might have become of Freddie? He might have fallen. Be lying hurt. And the fault was all hers. She should have stopped him running off like that.

At last, she stumbled onto the beach. Pulling herself up, she looked round, ignoring the sharp, searing pain in her ankle. And then it suddenly struck her. She felt her insides fall away. This was Gull Point, the very same beach where she'd nearly ended up stranded two years ago.

She turned and stared out to sea. It was impossible,

but it was true. These were the rocks where she'd tied the boat before the storm. And over there was where she'd gone for her walk. A rush of helplessness poured through her. How could fate be so cruel?

For in her mind this place spelled only one thing. Disaster.

But then something caught her eye. From just beyond the rocks, what appeared to be a small boat was heading towards her. Disbelievingly, she blinked. Surely she must be seeing things? It was the story of the wild flowers on the ledge all over again!

But it was still there when she looked again, and it was definitely coming closer. Then someone aboard was waving his arms at her. She stood transfixed as she heard him call out her name.

'Carla!'

It couldn't be. Horror glued her to the spot. I refuse to believe it, she thought. Please let this be a hallucination.

As the boat reached the shallows, she hadn't moved a muscle. She could see now that it was an inflatable dinghy with an outboard motor and she could also make out quite clearly who was on board. Though she'd already known, of course. Who else could it have been?

He jumped out and started to wade towards her. 'Are you okay?' The dark grey eyes were frowning. 'You look as though you've just seen a ghost.'

A ghost would have been better. Anything but Jedd. Tight-faced, Carla looked at him, wishing she could sink into the sand.

'Where did you come from?' she accused. 'How did you know I was here?'

'I always know where you are.' He stopped in front

of her and smiled. 'What's the matter? Aren't you pleased to see me?'

That was better not answered, and anyway he knew. It must be written all over her face what an absolute fool she felt.

But there were other, far more important things on her mind. 'We've got to get back up to the top of the cliff,' she told him. 'Freddie's gone missing. We've got to find him.' Sharply, she turned away, and very nearly keeled over at the excruciating pain that shot up her leg.

'What's the matter?' As she gasped, Jedd reached out and caught hold of her, then slipped an arm round her waist, taking her weight. 'You've hurt yourself. I knew it. Here, hang onto me.'

'It's nothing. Just my ankle. I twisted it on the way down.' She wanted to pull free but if she did she'd lose her balance and there was no way she could risk putting that foot on the ground again. As it was, the searing agony of it had brought tears to her eyes.

She breathed slowly. 'Just give me a minute. It'll pass. I'll be all right. Somehow, we have to get up there and look for—'

'No, we don't.' Before she could finish, he'd swept her up into his arms. Then, as she started to protest, he was setting her down on the sand, carefully arranging her injured foot in front of her. 'We don't have to go anywhere. Freddie's perfectly fine. Which is more than can be said for you. Let's have a look at that ankle.'

And he crouched down and started undoing the laces of her trainer.

Damned liberty! Carla glared at the top of his bent head. 'There's no need for this. And what do you mean Freddie's fine?'

'Just that.' Jedd paused to cast a quick glance up at her as, deftly and perfectly painlessly, he slipped off her shoe. 'He arrived back on his own shortly after you went after him. Apparently, Buster found him—instead of the other way round—and led him back to where Larry and the others were waiting.'

'Oh, thank God.' It was like a huge weight falling from her shoulders. 'And he's definitely okay? You're sure about that?'

'Not a scratch. You can stop worrying.' He was easing off her sock now. He frowned and shook his head. 'You've made a right mess of this.'

Carla looked down at her ankle, aware that it had stopped throbbing, feeling his fingers, cool and soothing, against the inflamed skin. She wondered if she should tell him just to leave it alone now, but decided against it. He seemed to know what he was doing.

She peered at the dark head. 'How come you know all about Freddie? And how did you know where to find me? You still haven't explained that.'

'I put two and two together. I knew where you'd left the road. And nobody could find you up on the cliff edge. So, I figured you'd come down and been unable to get back up again. I know from experience what that descent's like.'

He glanced up at her. 'By the way, this is just a sprain. Nothing's broken. Just sit there nice and still and I'll get a bandage wrapped round it.'

A bandage? Carla blinked as he pulled a roll of gauze from his pocket, squeezed out the excess sea water and began to wind it round the swelling. But she'd ask about that later. There were other mysteries to be cleared up first.

'How did you get here? Where did you get the boat? And how did you even know what had happened in the first place?'

He continued with what he was doing without answering for a moment. Carla watched him, following the rapid, gentle movements of his fingers, trying not to dwell too much on how pleasurable they felt.

'It was a fluke, really. I got back early and decided to join you. I knew more or less where you'd be, so I took the coast road for Gull Point and when I got near I called Larry on his mobile.'

He flicked her a quick smile. 'Talk about good timing. He told me the story of Freddie and Buster and how they were both back safely but that now you'd gone missing. He was just on the point of going after you himself, but I told him to stay put, that I'd find a way to get to you.'

Pausing for a moment, he tore the gauze into two strips and secured the bandage by tying the ends together. 'The quickest way here's by sea—that stretch of the road is notoriously slow—and by sheer coincidence there was a fishing boat just beyond the rocks. I got a message to them and asked if I could borrow a dinghy. Then I left the car and swam out to pick it up...'

He leaned back on his heels. 'And the rest you know.'

If anyone else had recounted such a story Carla would have thought they were making it up, but, coming from Jedd, it was all too easy to believe. It seemed to be in his character that he coped easily with crises. He kept his head, thought fast and acted decisively. And this was the second time she'd had reason to be grateful for that.

'Well, what can I say? Thank you,' she told him. As

she said it, it occurred to her that she was also rather glad that it was he who'd come to find her and not Larry.

But she'd no business thinking such things. Abruptly, she glanced away, wishing he'd stand up or, at the very least, move back a bit, instead of continuing to sit there right in front of her. This was all a little too intimate. Even her perfectly bandaged ankle seemed to proclaim a dangerous familiarity. And it didn't help at all as he smiled and told her, 'That's okay. It's all part of the service.'

Part of what service? She quelled a flicker of desire and decided it was time to put some distance between them. Inching back, she observed, 'Thank heavens about Freddie. I was almost going crazy worrying about him. If anything had happened, it would have been my fault.'

'Aren't you being a little hard on yourself?' Jedd frowned as he looked at her. 'From the story I heard, he didn't come back when you called him. It's hardly fair to blame yourself for that.'

'He's my responsibility. Of course I can blame myself.'

'Not entirely. He's a ten-year-old boy, not a helpless baby. I'd say he has to take some of the blame himself.' He paused. 'And anyway…allow me to correct you… strictly speaking, he wasn't your responsibility. Your colleague, Mrs Austen, was in charge, not you. You weren't even supposed to be there.'

'But I *was* there. That makes me responsible.'

Jedd laughed. 'You're incorrigible.' And he leaned forward and laid the backs of his fingers against her cheek.

Carla didn't know what to do. So she just sat very still, half wanting him to take his hand away, half praying that he wouldn't. All at once, she was alarmingly conscious of the fact that they were all alone together on this deserted stretch of beach. A slow pulse of excitement began to beat in her throat.

Eyes watching her, he dropped his hand lower to cup her chin. He seemed to be holding her there like a prisoner. The grey eyes scanned her face. Then suddenly he smiled. 'I wonder if you realise where you are?' he asked.

Oh, dear. Carla could feel the excitement in her quicken. Nervously, she swallowed and licked her dry lips. 'It's the same beach where I nearly got stranded that other time.'

That other time. To her own ears it sounded hopelessly provocative. She dropped her head as she said it, afraid to look him in the face.

He simply tilted her chin higher, forcing her to look at him. 'I think you do it on purpose. Go on. Confess. You come here deliberately so that I have to come and rescue you.'

As he smiled, Carla found herself smiling back. 'And you always just happen to be on hand when I need you. Maybe it's you who wills these situations so that you can come and play the hero.'

'You think I could will something like that?'

'It wouldn't surprise me.'

'Well, I must say, if I could, I'd probably do it more often.' His fingers tightened around her jaw a little. 'I rather enjoy coming to your rescue.'

As his gaze poured over her, Carla felt her stomach shrink. Oh, no. He's going to kiss me. She held her breath and said, 'You know, I think I maybe ought to be getting back now.'

'You really are incorrigible.' He smiled and shook his head, then slid his hand round to the back of her neck, making her shiver at the sensuous feel of his fingers. 'You're going nowhere,' he told her. 'The kids don't need you today. They've got someone else looking after them, remember? So, like it or not, for the moment you're staying here with me.'

Gently but firmly, he proceeded to pull her closer so that the only way she could balance was by laying her hands on his shoulders. She did so, very tentatively, his shirt wet beneath her fingers, and, instantly, a sharp, sweet longing pierced through her. With a small gasp, she closed her eyes, just as his lips crushed down on hers.

Jedd kissed the same way he did everything else. Without holding back. With intensity and passion. Carla clung to him, her fingers lacing into the slippery, damp hair, her mouth surrendering to his, no longer trying to resist. Why fight when she longed for the fire in him to consume her?

He was lowering her to the sand. It was warm against her back. Then his arms were winding round her and he was leaning over her, half on top of her. She arched her back to meet him, pressing against him, an almost unbearable hunger twisting through her.

As she gasped, one hand moved to the buttons of her blouse. In a trice, they were undone and he was pushing the blouse aside, then slipping his hand inside the cup of her bra. Carla shivered as his palm grazed the hard, thrusting peak, slowly, languorously, making her senses ache. Then he was pulling down the straps, setting her breasts free and bending to take one burning nipple in his mouth.

It was the most excruciating pleasure. Carla sank back, her body screaming for him. Never had she felt such intense longing for a man.

They lay there for a long time. Kissing. Caressing. Lost in the sweet, intimate discovery of one another's bodies. Carla stroked his broad chest, wishing they might both lose all self-control and allow their passion to carry them away. But, at the same time, she was glad he made no attempt to force the pace. It was too early for that. It would be better to wait.

At last, Jedd paused and looked down in her eyes. 'You know, the tide's coming in. If we stay here much longer, we're going to end up like that couple in *From Here to Eternity*, splashing about up to our necks in the waves.'

Carla laughed. That scenario rather appealed to her—the two of them as some latter-day Burt Lancaster and Deborah Kerr!

'Not that I'd mind,' Jedd was continuing, 'but maybe this isn't the right time...' He kissed her. 'I'm afraid, if we don't make a move soon, people are going to start wondering what's happened to us.'

Carla gazed into his face and was suddenly aware of a sensation of utter, perfect happiness, like a ray of golden sunshine curled around her heart. She smiled to herself. Something wonderful had happened and she and the world would never be quite the same again.

Jedd kissed her. 'So, I suggest that we make ourselves decent...' Caressing her breasts, he pulled her blouse shut. 'Just in case there are any sharp-eyed sailors out there. You never know what you're likely to encounter on the high seas.' He did up one of the buttons. 'Then I'll carry you out to the boat, for there's no way you can manage on your own with that ankle, and, without hurrying too much, we'll head back home.'

He dropped a quick kiss on her nose. 'How does that sound?'

Carla reached up and returned his kiss. She felt like pulling him down on the sand again, holding him tight and never letting him go.

'To be honest, it sounds like the last thing I feel like doing.' She pulled a face, then smiled resignedly. 'But you're right. We ought to get back.'

'Here we go, then.' Brushing the sand from his trousers, Jedd stood up. Then, in one quick movement, he scooped her into his arms, bending to deliver a teasing kiss on the lips. 'Now let's see if we can make it to the boat.'

Getting to the boat meant wading through knee-deep water that very rapidly rose to chest height. Carla giggled and twined her arms round his neck, then shrieked with helpless laughter as he suddenly dunked her up to her neck.

'Better to get it over with all in one go,' he laughed. 'There's nothing worse than letting it creep up on you gradually.'

'That's your story, you sadist!' She shook her dripping hair and kissed him. 'I can tell by the look on your face you enjoyed that.'

As they got nearer to the rocks where the dinghy was moored, the water became too deep to wade through.

'We'll have to swim the last part. Or, at least, *I'll* have to swim it.' Lowering himself, Jedd shifted her round onto his back. 'Hang on tight and I'll give you a piggyback. Just pretend I'm a dolphin or something.' Then he was setting off at a smooth, slow breaststroke through the waves.

Some dolphin! Carla rested her head between his shoulder-blades, loving the sensual feel of him moving beneath her and the warm, easy intimacy that had sprung up between them. Suddenly, everything was different. A sense of magic filled the air. Dreamily, she closed her eyes. If only it would never end.

As they finally reached the boat, Jedd stretched back to take her hand. 'Hang on tight to the side,' he told her, gently guiding her the last half-metre. Then he lifted himself up and over the edge of the dinghy, taking hold of her with both hands and heaving her up beside him before lowering her gently onto the wooden seat.

'Good girl. You made it. How does your ankle feel?'

'Wet.' Carla smiled at him. 'But, apart from that, it feels fine. I reckon that dip in the sea did it good.'

She sat back and watched as he yanked the engine into life, untied the mooring and guided the dinghy out to sea, and she didn't bother to fight the memories it conjured up. It was so different from that last time now. There was none of the tension. No thunder and lightning, no angry, pounding waves, just the two of them together on a sun-dappled sea. If that last time had been fire and brimstone, this was more like a taste of paradise.

Stretching her legs out in front of her, she glanced at her bandaged ankle and remembered that question she'd been meaning to ask him. She looked across at him with a smile as he sat steering the boat. 'Do you normally go around with rolls of gauze in your pocket, just in case you stumble upon some damsel with a twisted ankle?'

'Not normally, no.' Jedd met her smile with an amused look. 'But in this particular instance I thought it would probably be a good idea. It's not all that unusual for someone to do in their ankle coming down a cliff face without the right footwear. So I raided the first-aid box before I came ashore.'

He cast her a knowing smile. 'You remember about the first-aid box?'

Carla pulled a face. 'How could I forget?' Then she sighed. 'How come you always make me feel such an idiot? Compared to you, I'm just so utterly incompetent. First, I almost manage to get drowned in a storm, then I end up half-crippled and stranded on a beach. I shouldn't be let out. I'm a totally hopeless case.'

Jedd was watching her. He shook his head. 'You're inexperienced, that's all. You're not used to this environment. You're used to life in a big city. I've lived here virtually all my life. Of course I know the score—though, if you want to know the truth, I've been stranded before now too.'

Carla laughed. 'I don't believe you.'

'It's absolutely true. I was stuck once for a whole day before someone finally tracked me down. On this island it's easy, as you've discovered for yourself. If the cliffs don't get you, then the incoming tide will.'

He continued to watch her. 'And I'll tell you something else. I've had my fair share of near disasters with boats, especially when I was younger, with less respect for the elements. But I've learned, and you'd learn too if you stayed here for any time.'

Something flickered inside her. Half wish, half desire. How wonderful it would be if she really could remain here for a while. She'd love that. To have the opportunity to learn about the island. To discover all its secrets. To become a part of it. To belong. Though the thing she'd prize most would be the chance to really get to know Jedd.

The thought took her by surprise and, hurriedly, she turned away, afraid she might have blushed, though fearing something else much more—that he'd see what she was thinking and find it ridiculous.

She said lightly, to cover the confusion in her heart, 'So, you reckon that, with a bit of practice, I might eventually learn enough to go around saving people instead of always being the one who gets saved?'

As she met his eyes again, he gave her a long, thoughtful look. 'I reckon,' he said at last, 'that you'd be pretty good at saving.'

They arrived back far too soon and, as Carla spotted Pete, the marina assistant, waiting for them on the jetty, she was a little ashamed of the way her heart sank. They were back in the real world, their precious, private idyll over, though as Jedd smiled broadly and waved to the other man she instantly felt like a bit of an idiot. *He* obviously wasn't thinking any such foolish, romantic thing!

All the same, he seemed in no hurry to abandon her. In spite of Pete's offer to take her back to the castle, Jedd absolutely insisted on doing it himself.

He carried her to the waiting car and deposited her on the front seat. 'I'll take you up to your room,' he said, 'and you can rest that foot a while.' Then he was climbing in beside her and they were heading up the winding road and, though she knew she was being crazy, only one thought filled Carla's head. Where did they go from here? What was going to happen now?

Some twenty minutes later up in her room, he laid her gently on the bed. 'I'll tell Mrs Pickles you're here and explain what happened. Later, she can bring you some supper on a tray. For this evening, at least, I think you should stay put.'

He straightened and stepped back, then stood watching her for a moment, a sudden thoughtful frown shadowing his face. As Carla met the sober gaze, she felt a flutter of apprehension. *He regrets what happened between us. He's going to tell me it was a mistake.*

She couldn't bear to hear him say it. Quickly, she spoke. 'Please apologise to Mrs Pickles. I hate to put her out. But I don't think I could manage even one step right now.' For her ankle had started to throb painfully again as the anaesthesia of her earlier happiness wore off.

'No need for apologies. I'm sure Mrs Pickles won't mind.'

He paused, still with that worrying dark look in his eyes, and let his gaze flick over her unhurriedly for a moment. Nervously, Carla held her breath, but then, surprising her, he smiled.

'I think your bandage will do for now, but we can have a look at it later.' Then, making her heart stop, he leaned towards her and kissed her.

Carla had expected no more than a fleeting brush of his lips. But it was a proper kiss. Deep and slow and sexy. She felt a rush of huge relief. Her worries had all been in her head.

'I have to go now, but I'll see you later,' he promised. Then, with one last kiss, he moved away.

As he disappeared through the door, Carla leaned back against the headboard, her face a glowing pink picture of contentment.

* * *

'Who is it?'

Carla started as there was a knock on the bedroom door. She pulled herself up, shaking herself awake, for she'd been slumped against the pillows on the point of dozing off. Then she turned towards the door. 'Come in!' she called.

It must be Jedd, she decided, feeling a dart of excitement and giving her hair a quick fluff-up with her fingers.

But it wasn't Jedd at all. A small red head poked round the door. 'Can I speak to you, miss?' enquired a sombre-looking Freddie.

'Of course you can.' Carla smiled at him. 'What's the matter? Are you all right?'

'Yes, miss. I'm all right.' He came halfway to the bed and stopped. Carla had never seen such a serious look on a child's face. He took a deep breath. 'I've come to say I'm sorry. About your foot and all. About what happened. I know it was my fault.'

'Oh, Freddie, don't be silly. It doesn't matter. These things happen.' She frowned at him, feeling a rush of emotion in her heart.

'No, really. It was my fault. I should've listened when you called me. Then you wouldn't have come after me and ended up falling down the cliff.'

'I didn't fall down the cliff. I just stumbled, that's all. And my ankle will soon mend. I promise you it's nothing serious.'

'You're not angry, then?'

'Of course not. I'm just glad that you're safe. I confess you did give me a bit of a fright.'

'But you're not angry?'

'Don't be silly.'

'And you're not angry with Buster either? Jimmy and some of the other boys said it was all Buster's fault and that we wouldn't get to play with him or take him for walks any more. And it wasn't Buster's fault. He didn't know I'd go after him and I shouldn't have done anyway 'cos Jedd told us he wouldn't get lost 'cos he knows the whole island like the back of his paw. And he's a good dog. Really he is. It wasn't his fault.'

He came to a stop with a sob, finally running out of breath.

'Freddie, come over here.' Carla felt close to weeping herself. She held out her hand to him. 'There's no need to be upset.' Then, as at last he approached the bed, she caught hold of him and hugged him. 'Freddie. Freddie.' She kissed his head and stroked his hair. 'Of course I don't blame Buster and I know he's a good dog.'

For a moment, he just clung to her, pressing his face against her chest, until at last the storm of anguished sobbing was over. Using a corner of her sheet, Carla dabbed away his tears. She smiled at him and kissed him again. 'You really love Buster, don't you?'

'More than anything.' He wiped his nose with the back of his hand. 'I couldn't bear it if you were angry with him when I'm the one to blame.'

'Nobody's angry with him and of course you can play with him again. If you ask, I'm sure Jedd will let you take him for a walk tomorrow.'

'Mrs Pickles says I can feed him tonight.' For the first time, he smiled. 'He's got his own dish in the kitchen. She's going to show me what to do.'

'Then you'd better go and do it. He must be hungry, poor chap.'

'Usually, Jedd feeds him, but he's gone off somewhere with Larry.' Obviously quite restored, Freddie headed for the door. Then he stopped. 'You won't let Miss Jarvis find out what happened?' Miss Jarvis was Annie. 'She might be angry,' he explained. 'You never know. She might not understand.'

'I'm sure she would, you know, but I'll see it doesn't get back to her. Now off you go and don't worry about a thing.'

A moment later, he'd gone. Carla heard him scampering down the corridor as she leaned back against the pillows, a sudden heaviness in her heart.

So, Jedd had gone off with Larry. He wouldn't be coming, after all. Though that was probably a good thing, for what had she been thinking of today?

Until precisely thirty seconds ago, she'd entirely forgotten about Annie.

CHAPTER TEN

WHEN Jedd got back, it was already after midnight. He went into the kitchen and found Mrs Pickles, dressed in her long woolly red and green checked dressing gown, making her customary mug of bedtime cocoa.

'So, how's the invalid?' he asked, seating himself at the big refectory table and stretching his long, jeans-clad legs out in front of him.

'Sleeping, I hope. She certainly ought to be.' Mrs Pickles gave a cluck of good-natured disapproval as she lifted the pan of frothing milk from the Aga. 'Silly girl insisted on coming down to help with the children's supper, even though me and Lucy and Mrs Austen kept on telling her we could manage perfectly without her.' She tipped the milk into the mug and gave it a vigorous stir. 'Too conscientious by half, but she really loves these little boys and it's perfectly plain to see they just adore her.'

'Yes, I must say I'd noticed.'

Jedd cast her a warm smile. He happened to be enormously fond of Mrs Pickles, who was the most sensible, down-to-earth person he'd ever known. He'd even developed a bit of a soft spot for her Technicolor dressing gown over the years!

'So did Doc Milligan come to look at her ankle?' he asked. He'd phoned the doctor just before going off with Larry, even though he'd been pretty sure there wasn't really any need. It wouldn't do any harm to get a professional opinion.

Mrs Pickles pulled up a chair at the other side of the table 'He did. He gave her some pain-killers and strapped up her foot and told her to try and keep off it for a couple of days. But, like I said, as soon as he'd gone, she came hobbling downstairs insisting that she help with the children's supper. I could see she was determined, so I looked out Charlie's old walking stick and gave it to her to make it easier for her getting about.'

Jedd smiled at the image of Carla shuffling around the kitchen with the aid of Mrs Pickles' late husband's walking stick. 'So what time did she finally go off to bed?'

'Oh, not long after the boys, and they were off early tonight. Quite done in, they were, after their busy day out. I'd say it was just the back of ten o'clock.'

Jedd nodded. So there'd have been no point in trying to hurry back after all—though, as things had turned out, that would have been difficult anyway. It was a pity. He'd really wanted to speak to her tonight. After the unexpected turn things had taken this afternoon, it was suddenly rather important that he make a few things clear. Never mind. He'd have a word with her tomorrow—though he'd have to be very careful how he did it. There was a danger he might end up bruising her feelings.

He stretched his arms above his head and stifled a yawn. 'The boys aren't the only ones who're done in, I'm afraid. I reckon I'm ready to call it a day.'

'Shall I make you a cup of cocoa?'

'No, I won't need that tonight, thanks. I'll be asleep the second my head hits the pillow.' He stood up and went round to give her a quick peck on the cheek. 'Goodnight. See you in the morning.'

Then he went upstairs to bed.

Carla awoke feeling refreshed and astonishingly clear-headed, which was a vast improvement on how she'd felt last night.

Before she'd finally gone off to sleep, she'd lain for hours, just feeling miserable. She'd thought she'd found paradise, but she'd done nothing of the sort.

How could she have forgotten about Annie? What had she been thinking of? The way she'd behaved had been a total disgrace.

Still, there was one consolation. Her misery would soon pass. There was no way in the world she could go on wanting a man who was capable of betraying a girl as sweet as Annie. Jedd wasn't worth her pain. That was what she'd kept telling herself. Yet she'd continued to lie there in a fog of black despair.

This morning, however, when she opened her eyes, it felt as though the weight in her heart had lifted. This was her last day here. By evening, she'd be gone. And, besides, she knew exactly what she had to do. If Jedd tried any more moves, she'd tell him to get lost.

Even her ankle felt stronger as she hobbled along the corridor to wake the boys—Bertha had already gone back to St Orvel—though she had to lean quite heavily on Mrs Pickles' walking stick. And as she opened their bedroom door and was instantly greeted by a row of grinning faces and lusty chorus of, 'Good morning!' she immediately felt a hundred times better. *This* was what mattered. Who cared about cheats like Jedd?

Fortunately, there was no sign of him when they all

went down to the kitchen, where Mrs Pickles had already set the table for breakfast.

Carla gave her a stern look. 'Mrs Pickles, I said I'd do that. You really mustn't keep pampering me. I'm not an invalid, you know.'

'Hush. Just eat your corn flakes and stop complaining, young lady. Now hands up who's for orange juice. I've got some freshly squeezed in the fridge.'

The plan for the morning was that they'd go tree-spotting in the garden. Each boy would gather as many different leaves as he could find, then, with the help of Annie's nature book, they'd try to identify them. This suited Carla perfectly. She'd find herself a bench, prop up her bandaged foot on the little footstool Mrs Pickles had lent her and supervise the proceedings in comfort.

She'd barely settled herself, however, when there was a crunch of footsteps on the gravel path. She turned, her heart tightening, already guessing who it was.

'So I've finally managed to track you down!' Jedd looked relaxed and pleased to see her. He'd no idea that everything had changed.

Though perhaps not quite everything. Some things were still the same. For she'd been totally unable to control the emotion that poured through her the instant she'd looked into his face. It had felt like a nail driving into her heart.

She fought it as best she could. 'Hi,' she said lamely. The muscles in her cheeks felt painful and stiff.

'I'm glad you're on your own. I was hoping for a private word.' To Carla's horror, he proceeded to seat himself alongside her. As his arm brushed against hers, her whole body snapped tight.

Don't bother, she wanted to tell him. There's nothing

to talk about. But, though she opened her mouth, she couldn't get the words out.

'How's the foot?' He bent to study the appendage in question. 'I hear you had a visit from Dr Milligan last night. That's a much more professional-looking dressing you've got now.' And he raised his iron-grey eyes to hers and smiled.

It hurt to smile back at him. In a flash, she was re-membering how he'd tended her injured ankle on the beach. The way he'd astonished her by producing that roll of gauze from his pocket, the gentle touch of his hands as he'd wound it in place. There'd been magic in the air then, but now it was all gone.

She dropped her gaze away. 'It's much better today, thanks.'

There was a pause, then he said, 'Look, I'm really sorry about last night. I know I promised to drop by and see you, but I had to go and pick up the car from where I'd left it—'

As he broke off, it struck Carla that what was going through his head was that she was annoyed that he hadn't come and that was why she was acting strangely. She glanced up, her mind searching for the words to put him right, but, before she could say anything, he was carrying on.

'I'd hoped I'd be able to get back in time, but Larry came with me and when we got back he insisted that I go round to his house to see his new baby.'

'Larry's got a new baby?' In spite of herself, she smiled. 'I'd no idea. He's never said a word to me.'

'Her name's Bethany, she's a week old and she's the loveliest baby you ever saw. She looks just like her mother and she's the apple of her dad's eye.'

'Do they have any other children?'

'No, Bethany's their first. Though if the excitement in that house is anything to go by I predict she definitely won't be their last.'

'I should think not,' Carla laughed. 'They should have two or three, at least. I think there's nothing nicer than a house full of children.'

'Do you come from a big family?'

'No.' Carla shook her head. 'After me, my mother couldn't have any more. But I know, if she'd been able to, she'd have had three or four.'

'I was an only child, too.' His eyes scanned her face. 'But, like you, I've always fancied a house full of kids.'

There was something in his gaze that made Carla glance away. An intense, probing intimacy which was quite out of place. His paternal ambitions were of no interest to her and all it did was irritate her that he shared her feelings about such things. Over the last couple of minutes, she'd started to relax, but now she felt herself tense again and inwardly draw away from him. Why in heaven's name had she allowed herself to get pulled into this conversation?

'Carla.' Suddenly, he was laying his hand on her arm. 'There's something I want to tell you. Something you ought to know.' As her eyes snapped up to look at him, he was about to carry on, but at that precise moment Freddie came haring towards them along the gravel path.

'Look what I've found! Look what I've found!' He was brandishing one closed fist. 'I was looking for leaves and it was hidden under a hedge!'

As he skidded to a halt in front of them, two thoughts shot through Carla's head. One, that she felt like kissing him for his impeccable timing. Two, that she wasn't at all sure she wanted to see what he'd found.

'Before you show me,' she said, 'please just tell me how many legs it's got.'

She heard Jedd laugh as, to her relief, he withdrew his hand from her arm. 'Perhaps you'd better show it to me first,' he suggested. 'I'm not so squeamish about legs.'

'It hasn't got any legs.' Freddie was catching his breath. Then, proudly, with a flourish, he held out his hand. 'Look!' he invited. 'It's Buster's name tag.'

'So it is.' Jedd picked up the blackened copper disc. 'He lost it a couple of months ago. I had to get him a new one.' He reached out and affectionately ruffled the child's hair. 'If you like, you can keep it. As a souvenir.'

Freddie's eyes grew round with pleasure. 'Do you mean that? Can I really?' And, in spite of her rather mixed feelings about Jedd at the moment, it struck Carla that that was the nicest thing he could have done.

She smiled at Freddie. 'See how lucky you are? I think you'd better say thank you to Jedd.'

'Thank you.' His fingers had closed tightly round the disc. 'Thank you,' he said again. 'I'll keep it for ever.'

Jedd rose to his feet. 'I think I'd better leave you.' He smiled down at Freddie. 'Be sure and keep that tag safe, now.' Then he turned to face Carla. 'And you look after that foot.' As he said it, he reached out and very briefly touched her cheek. 'I'll speak to you later. Maybe after lunch.'

Then he turned and went striding off across the gravel, leaving Carla sitting asking herself what had happened to her tongue.

*　　*　　*

It was a couple of hours later and Carla and her charges were heading back to the castle kitchen for lunch. The children were running ahead, armed with their bags of leaves and Annie's nature book, as well as Mrs Pickles' needlepoint footstool. Carla and her walking stick were doing their best to keep up.

As she limped along, she was thinking of Jedd and wondering what he could possibly want to tell her, though she'd decided it was almost certainly something to do with Annie.

A confession, perhaps? No, confessions weren't his style. An attempt to play down his relationship with her friend? Or a request for her to keep quiet about his tendency to stray? She had a feeling it was probably one of the last two.

Well, I don't want to know, she thought to herself angrily. She'd no wish to hear his lies and it would just be too insulting if he were to suggest there was some danger she might go blabbing to Annie about what had happened. So, she'd keep out of his way and maybe he'd get the message. She really wasn't interested in hearing anything he had to say.

The boys had disappeared into the kitchen, with Carla only a few steps behind them, when Henrietta's open-top sports car suddenly appeared. Carla stopped and turned towards it. This was the first time she'd seen Henrietta since that unfortunate encounter outside Jasper's room last week when she'd offered Carla money to take Nicholas's side against Jedd. Carla had already decided her friend must have taken temporary leave of her senses and that the best policy was just to act as though the incident had never happened, so as the car began to slow down she smiled and stepped towards it.

But the strangest thing happened. Henrietta fixed her with a black glare. 'Bitch!' she spat, and then went speeding off.

Carla stumbled back, startled, as the car disappeared in a cloud of dust. What in heaven's name was *that* about? Quite clearly, she'd flipped again!

Though, in the very same instant, another thought occurred to her. She'd decided it was unfair of her to suspect that Henrietta might have deliberately lied about Jedd. Now she wasn't so sure. She'd just had perfect proof of a not quite so appealing side to her friend's character that up until now she'd somehow missed!

It was an hour or so before teatime and the children were down at the stables. Carla hurried along the corridor, heading for Jasper's room. She'd promised to pop in and say goodbye before she left and, since Larry was taking them over on one of the launches at five-thirty, this was probably the last chance she'd get.

She'd brought him a little farewell gift—though, of course, she'd be seeing him again. A bottle of his favourite port, which she'd got Lucy to buy in St Orvel. She'd wrapped it in some pretty paper and tied on a yellow bow, and she was clutching it in her hand as she headed towards his door.

This morning, when she'd dropped in to see him after breakfast, he'd been looking brighter than she'd seen him for ages. Almost the old Jasper she remembered from two years ago. He'd been sitting up in bed chatting away happily, virtually running the conversation by himself. Seeing him so much better had given Carla a huge lift. It surely wouldn't be too long now before he was back on his feet.

Her tap on the door elicited a loud, 'Come on in!' And, as she started to turn the handle, Carla smiled to herself. That definitely hadn't been the voice of a man destined to be bedbound for very much longer!

'Hi, there. It's me.'

She pushed the door open and stepped inside—and very nearly dropped the bottle of port. For sitting in his usual chair on the other side of the bed was Jedd.

It was just like that first time. She stared in horror for a moment. She'd been absolutely certain that, just ten minutes before, she'd seen him disappearing off down the drive in the Land Rover.

Inwardly, she cursed. Why did this have to happen, just when she'd been making such a good job of avoiding him?

Earlier, as she and Lucy had been clearing up after lunch, she'd glanced out of the window and seen him approaching.

'Excuse me, I have to get something from my room,' she'd told the other girl, and, feeling thoroughly ashamed of herself, had disappeared upstairs for ten minutes.

Later, on her way to join the boys in the garden, she'd spotted him again, off in the distance, but definitely heading in her direction, and had actually left the path and hidden behind a tree. She knew it was pathetic and she'd felt like a total lunatic, but the thought of being confronted with him on her own totally appalled her.

And now here he was, and this time she was stuck—though at least, thank heavens, they weren't alone.

'Nice to see you. Come in and sit down,' he told her. And though his tone revealed nothing it was perfectly obvious that he was trying to figure out what had caused her strange reaction. The smile that had initially greeted her had been replaced by a curious frown.

Carla nodded to him quickly before crossing to the old man and greeting him warmly with a kiss on the cheek as she sat down on the bed and laid the bottle on the nearby armchair. I'm here for your uncle, so please stay out of my hair, every stiff, rejecting movement of her body was trying to warn him.

Just like this morning, Jasper was on top form.

He chatted away happily and asked her lots of questions about the boys. 'I want to meet these young charges of yours,' he told her. 'But not just yet. Once I'm up and about. An old man's sickroom is no place for children.'

'You'd enjoy meeting them. I'm sure of it. They're a really lovely bunch. And I'll bet it won't be long before you *are* up and about. As I've already told you, you're looking great today.'

'I feel great.' With a conspiratorial frown, he leaned towards her. 'Between you and me, if it wasn't for Jedd here, I'd have been up giving my old legs a bit of stretch this afternoon.'

'It's a bit early for that, Uncle.' Jedd spoke at last. He'd been sitting very quietly up until now, leaving all the talking to Jasper and Carla. 'I know you're much better,' he continued. 'It wouldn't be wise to take things too fast.' He paused. 'I'm sure Carla would agree with that…wouldn't you, Carla?'

Carla knew it was a ploy to make her turn and look at him, for she hadn't so much as glanced at him since she'd sat down. A little awkwardly, she swivelled round and felt hot colour flood her cheeks at the sheer intensity of the expression on his face.

'I think you're probably right,' she said. Her heart had begun to race and she was aware of a swift, painful plummet of regret for the decision she'd had no choice but to make. It was still true that she'd never felt such strong emotion for any man.

She turned abruptly back to Jasper. 'It's probably sensible to take things slowly. You don't want to risk undoing all the progress you've made.'

The old man sighed and sat back with a resigned smile against the pillows. 'I knew it. I'm outnumbered. Okay, I'll do as I'm told.'

Soon, it was time for Carla to go.

She squeezed the old man's hand. 'I'm afraid I've got to leave you. The boys will be back from their riding lesson soon and I have to get them cleaned up and looking their best for Mrs Pickles' special farewell tea.' She stood up. 'But I'll be back soon. Probably in a couple of days. In the meantime, just look after yourself and keep on getting better.'

Conscious of Jedd's eyes on her—though she didn't even glance at him—she headed towards the door and quickly snatched it open. Then she was stepping out into the corridor, praying he wouldn't follow her, pulling the door shut and heading for the stairs.

She'd gone only about five steps when she heard the door open again behind her.

'Carla! Can I have a word?'

She forced herself to stop. 'Of course.' And she turned with a wooden smile to face him.

As he came striding towards her, suddenly he smiled. 'I seem to be forever chasing you down this corridor. It's your fault for always being in such a hurry to leave.' He halted a couple of metres away. 'But don't worry. I won't keep you. I know you have to get back to the boys.'

Carla nodded, struggling hard to control the anxiety that was suddenly pressing like a closed fist inside her. And as she looked into his face she immediately understood why it was that she'd been so terrified to confront him alone.

One to one, face to face, he was so hard to resist. She felt thrown into confusion, her feelings tangled and blurred. It would take only one glance, one touch, one kiss and she'd instantly forget the promise she'd made herself. As it was, that quick smile had almost knocked it from her head.

He peered down at her. 'I've been trying to get hold of you all afternoon.' As he paused, something flickered at the back of his eyes. A shadow of suspicion? But then it was gone. He smiled at her again. 'Unfortunately, I keep missing you.'

Carla faked a surprised look. 'Oh, really?' she said.

'I'd have joined you for tea, but I've got some paperwork that won't wait.' He shook his head wryly. 'My very favourite task. But I want to see you off and have a word before you go.' He reached out and touched her cheek. 'What time are you leaving?'

Perhaps, if he hadn't done that, she'd have told him the truth. But as her heart flared with excitement Carla was suddenly filled with panic. She took a quick breath. 'The launch is picking us up at six,' she said.

'Okay. I'll be down at the marina in plenty of time.' He took a step back. 'Off you go now.' He smiled. 'And I hope you and the boys enjoy your tea—though I'd be grateful if you'd ask them to leave at least one scone for me.'

Carla managed a weak smile back. 'Of course I will,' she said. Then she turned away quickly and fled down the stairs.

What on earth was happening to her? She didn't know herself any more. One minute she was doing weird things like hiding behind trees and now she was coming out with the most appalling, barefaced lies.

The launch left on time, at five-thirty on the dot.

Seated in the back, surrounded by her charges, Carla was having to struggle to make some pretence of sharing their excitement about the journey ahead. She was glad they were on their way, of course, but she felt all tight and numb inside—and deeply uncomfortable about that lie, which had continued to gnaw away relentlessly in her mind. It had totally ruined Mrs Pickles' fabulous tea for her. For appearances' sake, she'd forced down a couple of scones, but, for all she'd tasted, she might as well have eaten her napkin.

All the same, what she'd done had been for the best. As the launch set sail with no sign of Jedd on the marina, Carla told herself that the only thing she felt was relief.

But if that was really true how on earth did she explain the cold, empty hole where her heart used to be?

CHAPTER ELEVEN

JEDD was driving down the hill, heading for the marina, when through a gap in the trees he saw the launch move away.

He cursed. Surely not? And he glanced at his watch, wondering if he'd read it wrongly before and really was late. But, just as he'd thought, it was only twenty-five to six. Either Larry had decided to leave half an hour ahead of schedule or Carla had made a mistake.

Though there was a third possibility. She'd told him the wrong time on purpose.

Well, there was definitely no point in going any further. He drew up at the roadside and sat watching for a moment as the gap between the launch and the marina wall widened. Of the three possibilities, somehow that last one seemed most likely.

It all added up. The strange way she'd been acting. The suspicion he'd had that she was deliberately avoiding him. He'd tried telling himself he was imagining it, but he hadn't really been convinced, and now it was obvious that his intuition had been right. In her discreet, subtle way, she'd been giving him the brush-off.

Very well, then. Point taken. He slipped the engine back into gear, did a quick, impatient U-turn and headed back up the hill. If that was the way she wanted it, that was the way it would be. Though it might have been nice if she'd taken the trouble to explain why.

'I guess that's just the way it goes.' He glanced at

Buster through the rear-view mirror as the dog sat in the back seat wagging his tail. 'You just never can tell how things are going to turn out.'

He frowned to himself. It didn't matter a damn, of course, and the wise thing to do would be just to write her off. She'd be leaving in a few weeks anyway, stepping out of his life for good, and he'd known he'd no business getting involved with her in the first place. But the truth was he was curious. He'd actually like to find out what lay at the root of this rather abrupt turnaround. Could there possibly be some connection with what he'd been planning to talk to her about?

Forget it, he told himself. You've more important things to do than waste your time worrying about that. She didn't want to listen, so let's just leave it. As he turned into the castle grounds, he switched his mind to other things.

'Come on, Buster, let's go and see if there are any of those scones left.'

'Welcome back! How are you feeling? How's your poor ankle?'

Back at the Starship Centre, Annie and the other children were waiting in the garden for Carla and the boys when their minibus finally drew up outside the gates. As the two girls went inside, leaving the children to go off to play, Annie took Carla's arm and gave her a warm hug. 'My, you've really been in the wars!'

Carla smiled at her. 'It's much better now. It hardly hurts at all.'

'Good. But you ought to rest it, so let's go and sit down. Besides, I want to hear all about what you've been up to.'

Well, maybe not all. Carla thought guiltily of Jedd, who, throughout the journey home, hadn't been out of her mind for a second. He seemed to have taken up permanent residence in her brain.

She'd soon put a stop to that, though. There was nothing to think about. It was over. Finished. And the only question that should be troubling her was how she could ever have betrayed Annie in the first place. She was the last person to deserve such a treacherous friend. It was bad enough that she already had a faithless boyfriend.

As she allowed herself to be propelled into the kitchen and sat down, Carla glanced at Annie and put up a silent prayer. Whatever else happens, don't let her find out. I really couldn't bear to see her hurt because of me.

It was a huge relief to get back to the old routine.

Over the next few days, Carla threw herself into work. This was what she cared about, what made her life sweet. The Jedd thing had just been a frivolous, passing nonsense. And it was only a matter of time before she finally swept him from her system.

For, alas, she hadn't quite managed to do that yet. Frequently, unexpectedly, he'd jump into her head. She'd see his face, recall his smile, remember something he'd said and be filled with a helpless, intense sense of loss. She knew she was being silly, but she just couldn't help it.

And then there was Annie's surprise revelation.

Soon after she got back, Carla asked her what on earth had suddenly prompted her to give her that day off.

'It was Jedd,' Annie replied, making her blink in surprise. 'He phoned me that morning early, before breakfast, and told me you'd been up again with Freddie the night before and that you were looking tired and needed a rest.' She frowned. 'That was naughty of you. You should have told me yourself.'

'But I was managing fine. I didn't need a day off.' It was true that she did sometimes feel a little tired, but when Freddie, or any of the other kids, needed her she always managed to find the energy from somewhere. 'Jedd had no business phoning you,' she protested.

Jasper, she decided, must have told him about Freddie's nightmares, but how had he known about the one the previous night? He must have been spying on her. How dared he? she thought angrily. Though what on earth had possessed him to report back to Annie like that?

His interfering nature, that's all! she told herself sharply. So don't bother kidding yourself it was anything else! It would be highly unwise to start imagining hidden meanings. The task of forgetting him was already hard enough.

She went twice to visit Jasper, who just looked better all the time, and on neither occasion was there any sign of Jedd. It would appear he'd got the message. Well, that was a relief.

There was only one dark cloud. Poor little Freddie. The relaxed child he'd been briefly during those days on Pentorra had vanished. Once more, he'd gone back to his difficult, withdrawn ways.

'What's the matter?' Carla had asked him, though she'd suspected she knew the answer.

And she'd felt her heart weep as he'd raised sad eyes and said, 'Do you think Jedd might bring Buster over to visit us one day?'

She'd taken hold of him and hugged him. 'I think he might. We'll ask Annie.'

And that was how she knew—for she had spoken to Annie—that Jedd was planning a visit to the centre the following day.

For Freddie's sake, she was glad, of course. For herself, she felt scared. Her instant reaction at the thought of seeing him again had not been at all what it ought to have been. She'd felt a flare of quick excitement, a tightness round her heart—and not a shadow of the indifference she'd been struggling so hard to feel.

It's hopeless, she thought. As soon as I see him, I'll be back to square one.

But forewarned was forearmed. She'd keep out of his way. She knew from Annie that he'd be coming during the children's free playtime, so she'd disappear off to her room and write some letters or something.

Next day, true to her promise, having heard the Land Rover draw up, Carla was halfway up the stairs before he'd even stepped down onto the pavement. A couple of minutes later, she was standing by her open bedroom window listening to the squeals of pleasure as he joined the children in the garden and smiling at Freddie's ecstatic 'Buster! Buster!' But she didn't look out. Quite frankly, she didn't dare. Just seeing him might unravel her fragile control.

She sat down at her little desk and picked up her pen. Put him out of your mind! she commanded herself. Concentrate on something else! She pulled her notepad from the drawer. Now get writing those letters!

The children had moved round to the other side of the garden. Outside, it was quiet. Nothing to distract her. And she was doing quite well. She'd written a couple of pages. But then, behind her, the door suddenly opened.

Carla started and spun round. A rush of hot and cold went through her. 'What are you doing here? Kindly get out!'

Jedd ignored that invitation and, closing the door behind him, stepped forward to face her from the middle of the carpet. 'I'm sorry to disturb you.' He plainly meant not a word. 'But there's something I have to say to you. I need a few minutes of your time.' Then he went and seated himself on the edge of her bed.

'Where's Annie? Does she know you're here?' It was the first thought that had crossed her mind. Wouldn't it just be perfect if Annie were to walk in on them now?

Jedd fixed her with a narrow look. 'Yes, I told her I wanted to see you. She said I'd probably find you here.'

And what on earth must she be thinking? Carla felt a twinge of guilty panic. She had a vision of Annie pacing about suspiciously downstairs. 'Well, just say what you have to say—as quickly as possible—then leave.'

'Don't worry, I don't intend staying any longer than I need to.' There was a harsh edge to his voice. 'This is purely a duty visit. You needn't be afraid that I'm here for anything else.'

'Well, that's a relief.' She hoped her tone was as cold as his. Just for a moment there, like an idiot, she'd felt hurt.

He sat back on the bed. 'I wasn't going to bother. Quite frankly, it's all a bit irrelevant now anyway. But for my own peace of mind I'd like to set the record straight. Probably, I should have spoken before we—' As he broke off, Carla knew he was referring to that episode on the beach. Then he shrugged. 'But, anyway, I'm telling you now.'

Carla stared back at him. What was he about to come out with? If it was something to do with Annie, maybe she should tell him to save his breath? But then he said, 'It concerns my feelings for you.'

It was shocking the way her stomach instantly dissolved. Suddenly, for a moment, everything seemed possible again. She felt a crushing rush of misery. If only that were so.

She said, as though to punish herself, 'Well, that shouldn't take long.'

Jedd looked back at her in silence. A minute ticked by. Then he sighed. 'The first thing I want to do is apologise.'

'Apologise?'

'In the past, I had a very low opinion of you and made no particular effort to hide it. But I realise now I was totally wrong. I did you a very grave injustice. You're not the girl I used to think you were at all.'

It was funny hearing him say it, for it was only as she listened that Carla realised she'd already figured that out for herself. Not consciously, but deep inside, she'd been aware of this shift in him. It was a while since she'd seen that old look of contempt.

'So, that's why I was allowed to visit Jasper on my own? You finally understood I wasn't about to fleece him, after all? I'd thought maybe it was just because you couldn't spare the time.'

'No, I'd changed my mind.'

'And what made you do that?' There was anger in her voice as all the old insults came back to her. 'Though, actually, what I'd *really* like you to explain is where your bad opinion of me came from in the first place.'

Jedd looked at her and shook his head. 'I don't think we need to go into that.'

'Don't you? Well, I'm sorry, but I think we do. Tell me. I got the impression you thought you *knew* something about me.'

He said nothing for a moment, just narrowed his eyes, and suddenly Carla sensed there was a battle going on inside his head. 'Maybe,' he said at last as he seemed to come to a decision. 'But I'm afraid that's all I'm going to say on the matter.'

'Oh, no, it's not! I demand an explanation!'

Again he shook his head. 'I'm not prepared to give one.'

Carla was growing angry. She turned to face him more squarely. 'I think you've got a nerve. You behaved abominably towards me. You accused me of all sorts of vile, disgusting things. And now you come here pretending to apologise, but at the same time making it plain that you had a reason for your bad opinion... That isn't an apology It's just another insult in disguise!'

She paused, catching her breath. 'You *owe* me an explanation!'

'Why are you insisting?' There was impatience in his voice. 'Isn't it enough that I've admitted unreservedly that I was wrong?'

'No, it's not. Not at all. I want to know where it all came from. Why are you so reluctant to tell me?'

'Because you wouldn't like it.'

'And what is that supposed to mean?' She glared at him, furious now. 'I insist that you tell me. There's no way I'm letting you off with a statement like that!'

Jedd released a hissing sigh, full of pent-up irritation, but there was an expression of reluctant resignation on his face.

'Okay, you asked for it.' He looked her straight in the eye. 'It was Nicholas who told me you were a gold-digger.'

It was like a slap in the face. Carla felt herself recoil. 'That's a lie! Nicholas never told you any such thing!'

'I warned you you wouldn't like it.' He sighed again and frowned, and there was pain and bitterness in his tone as he went on, 'That time you came here on holiday he told me certain things about you. He said you'd virtually cleaned him out financially, that you were always demanding gifts and holidays. But he was in love with you and desperately didn't want to lose you, so he asked if I could lend him some money.'

Carla felt herself turn cold. 'That's a lie,' she insisted. She only just managed to get the words out.

'Later, when you split up, he told me he'd got rid of you because he'd finally had enough and come to his senses. But he was broke again, thanks to you, and needed another loan.'

'I don't believe you. How could he?' Every inch of her was trembling. 'It was never like that. I never asked him for anything. It was him who always insisted on splashing money around.'

'Yes, I know.' Jedd sighed again and closed his eyes for a moment. 'As I got to know you better, I gradually came to realise that he must have been lying, that not a word of it was true. I'm sorry I ever believed him, but he's my cousin, after all, and though we've never been close I suppose I feel a certain loyalty. At the time, it never occurred to me that he was making it up.'

Carla was sitting very still, struggling to hold herself together. Now she understood Henrietta's offer of money. She'd obviously been told the same stories as Jedd. Then a new horror occurred to her. 'Did he tell Jasper all this stuff, too?'

'Not a chance.' A dark, cynical look touched Jedd's eyes. 'There's no way he'd have wanted Jasper to think he was financially incompetent. At that time, he was still in line for a share of the estate.'

He rose from the bed and started to come towards her. 'No, it was always me he used to borrow from—loans, needless to say, that were never paid back. Not long before you came on the scene, I'd told him it had to stop and had actually turned him down a couple of times.'

As he came to stand before her, he reached out and cupped her chin. 'I can see now that was why he came up with the gold-digger story. It was an attempt to win my sympathy. He knew I'd be vulnerable to that.'

At the touch of him, Carla could feel the blood flow back into her veins. 'Why?' she said, looking up into his face.

Jedd smiled a wry smile. 'Because of my past.' With his fingertips he softly caressed her jaw and throat. 'You see, I was involved once with a woman like that. A youthful folly. I was in my early twenties. She was a lot older and I was totally besotted. She ended up taking me for virtually every penny I possessed—which, fortunately, wasn't actually a huge amount of money.'

He sighed. 'Still, it was a lesson I've never forgotten. It made me wary—and possibly inclined to be too suspicious.' He reached down and took her hand, gently drawing her to her feet. 'I'm really sorry my bad experience ended up rebounding on you. You're the last person in the world anyone could ever accuse of being like that.'

'Unless you're Nicholas, it would seem.'

'Forget Nicholas. He's not worth it. Any man who could tell such lies about a girl like you doesn't deserve to be given a second thought.' He tipped her chin and frowned deep into her eyes for a moment. 'I wouldn't blame you if you thought the same about any man who believed them.'

Carla smiled a weak smile and slowly shook her head. 'I'm sorry you believed them, but I can understand why. Your cousin is obviously a bit of an expert at deception. Look at me. Not for a moment did I ever suspect that he might be capable of something like that. I'd say he did a pretty good job of fooling us both.'

'Does that mean you forgive me?' He squeezed her hand as he spoke. The look in his eyes was dark and intense.

It really mattered to him that she did. Carla felt a warm rush inside. 'Yes,' she said, meaning it. 'I think that it does.'

For the first time, he smiled, though it was a smile full of remorse. 'Thank heavens for that.' He took hold of her and held her. And for a moment he just stood there, arms wrapped round her tightly, his face buried in her hair, as though he'd never let her go.

Carla remained very still, listening to his breathing, feeling as though some barrier around her heart had finally fallen. It was like that moment on the beach when she'd looked into his face and experienced a sensation of utter, perfect happiness, only now it was a thousand times more intense.

She laid her cheek against his chest, drinking in the

scents of him. I love him, she thought. I really do love him. To acknowledge it felt like the most wonderful release.

He kissed her hair, then drew away a little, gazing down into her eyes. 'If you'd known all this a few days ago,' he asked softly, 'would you still have lied to me about what time the launch was leaving?'

It was like being snapped out of a dream. Carla felt herself freeze. Once again, she'd entirely forgotten about Annie.

Suddenly numb, she stepped back, withdrawing her hand from his. It was too cruel. She felt like weeping. But she forced herself to speak.

'I'm sorry about that lie. It was cowardly of me, and stupid. I should have had the guts to tell you to your face... But it's out of the question that there can be anything between us. What happened was a mistake. I don't know what got into me. I'm really not the sort of girl—'

She'd been about to add 'who goes around stealing other women's men'. But she didn't have a chance. Jedd was cutting in.

'Okay. I've heard enough.' He held up his hand to silence her. Suddenly, a closed look had fallen across his face. 'I'm sorry, but naturally I respect the way you feel.' He gave a quick, oddly formal little nod of the head, then turned on his heel and strode towards the door. 'I guess I'd better be going. I'll see you around.'

A moment later, he snatched the door open and was gone.

Carla nearly ran after him. She had to fight not to cry out. How could she let him go? Especially now. And like this.

But she had to. And it was better this way. Now

there'd be no more misunderstandings. No more fear of betraying Annie. Now she could live with herself.

She turned away and closed her eyes, tears choking in her throat. Okay, so she could live at peace with herself now, but how on earth was she going to live without Jedd?

'Come on. Let's have a glass of wine and relax for five minutes. I don't know about you, but I feel totally whacked tonight.'

The children were asleep, the rest of the staff had gone to their rooms and Carla and Annie were alone in the kitchen, Annie brandishing a bottle of best New Zealand Chardonnay as she looked out two glasses and laid them on the table.

Carla nodded. 'Okay.' Actually, she'd rather have gone to bed. Since Jedd's abrupt exit from her room and from her life, she'd literally been feeling worse by the minute. Her heart weighed inside her like a lump of cold lead.

She'd waited till she was certain the Land Rover had driven off before she'd dared to come downstairs. Then she'd busied herself with the children, struggling to keep her mind a blank. Though, of course, it hadn't worked. Jedd was there in her every thought.

Still, maybe the wine might help. It might numb the ache a bit. She sat down as Annie filled the two glasses to the brim and pushed one of them across the table towards her.

'You're right, it's been a very long day.' She forced what she hoped was a light-hearted smile. 'But one of us, at least, didn't have any complaints. I've never seen any child look as happy as Freddie when I went to tuck him up tonight. And he just couldn't stop talking about Buster.'

'Yes, I noticed the transformation. He's really crazy about that dog.' Annie paused and suddenly leaned across the table with a curious look. 'That was a long conversation you had earlier with Jedd.'

Carla nearly spilled her wine. What an idiot she was! Why had she brought Buster into the conversation? Though there was something in Annie's expression that made her suspect she'd probably have got round to the subject of Jedd anyway. Maybe Jedd was what this little get-together was really all about.

'It was nothing important. I don't know why he bothered.' She shrugged, praying she'd managed to sound detached and reassuring, though she had a horrible suspicion she'd actually done the opposite and had simply given the impression she was hiding something.

Clearly, she had.

'Is something going on between you and Jedd?' Annie frowned and fixed her with a penetrating look.

'Of course not. Don't be silly. Whatever made you think that?'

'I've thought it for a while. Ever since you came back from Pentorra. Earlier than that, really. More or less right from the start.'

'Good heavens, you're crazy!' Carla fiddled nervously with her glass, wishing the floor would open up and swallow her. 'Nothing's going on. Nothing. I promise you.'

Annie subjected her to a long look. 'I'm sorry, I don't believe you. If you ask me, this is a case of the lady protests too much.' And then, to Carla's astonishment, her face broke into a smile. 'Go on. Tell me the truth. You're having a thing with him, aren't you?'

Why on earth was she smiling? Carla blinked in total bafflement. Why wasn't she doing something normal, like leaping across the table and throttling her? She sat frozen in her seat, at a total loss as to how to respond.

'I'd be happy for you if you were. Jedd's a very special guy. To be honest with you, I once had quite a fancy for him myself. But we're not really each other's type. We could never be more than friends.'

Carla was aware that she was staring at Annie as though she'd suddenly grown two heads. Any second I'm going to wake up and discover this was all a dream, she thought. She forced herself to speak. 'Is that all you are, then? Just friends?'

'Of course. What did you think?' Suddenly Annie shrieked with laughter. 'You're the one who's crazy. Of course we're just friends!'

Carla resisted the urge to pinch herself. Inside, she was singing. 'But he's always phoning you up and dropping round to see you. And what about those meetings at the Partridge Inn?'

'All perfectly innocent. Definitely not what you were thinking—though I can see how you managed to get the wrong impression. These little get-togethers of ours are strictly business.

'Oh, dear—' Annie broke off and clapped her hand guiltily over her mouth. 'I shouldn't have said that. It's supposed to be a secret.'

'What's supposed to be a secret?' Carla wanted to know everything now! 'Come on,' she demanded. 'Out with it. Explain!'

'Okay—if you promise to keep it to yourself. Jedd

doesn't like people knowing about his connection with the centre—which is why I had to be so mysterious about everything in the first place.'

She paused. 'The Starship Centre actually belongs to Jedd. It's his brainchild; he set it up and he provides the money to run it.'

'Jedd?' Carla was aware that her mouth had dropped open. Surely Annie was pulling her leg?

But apparently not. She was continuing in a serious tone, 'He leaves the day-to-day running of things to me. I select the children and do all the hiring and firing, but he's very involved with the various activities that go on. He helps set up the courses and the outings and things like that. Policy stuff—and, of course, he runs the financial side. And he's terribly generous, as you've seen for yourself. We don't lack for anything. We've got all the resources we need.'

Carla sat back with a sigh. 'I'm astounded. I never suspected.' Suddenly, she was recalling how, on her very first visit, Jasper had made some comment about Jedd being involved with the centre. She hadn't believed it—even before Jedd had denied it—for at that time she'd been certain he wouldn't be interested in something like that. Well, how utterly, totally wrong could you be?

A thought suddenly struck her. 'But I don't understand. I'd no idea Jedd had that sort of money.'

'Most people have no idea, but the truth is he's loaded. When he was in his late twenties he made a fortune from property, then his parents died tragically a couple of years ago and literally left him millions.

'But he doesn't flash it around and he spends hardly anything on himself. No fancy cars or jet-setting about.

That's not what Jedd's into. He's much happier, if you ask me, using his money to try and help others.'

Carla was having trouble taking this in. She said, half to herself, 'In that case, it definitely makes no sense at all that he'd bother persuading his uncle to make him sole heir to the estate.'

'Who told you that? Was it Henrietta, by any chance?' As Carla nodded, Annie frowned and shook her head. 'She and Nicholas went mad when Jasper changed the will. They really behaved disgracefully, trying to get him to change it back again. And now they've definitely got it in for Jedd.

'Neither of them have any idea about his money, by the way. They come from two sides of the family who know virtually nothing about each other. They're aware he's worth a few thousand, but no more than that.'

She smiled. 'Jedd's never cared about the inheritance—at least not as far as the money's concerned. But he loves Pentorra. He's made it what it is. Jasper did the right thing when he decided to change his will. Leaving the estate to be run jointly between the two cousins would never have worked. And Nicholas hasn't been left out. He'll get a fair chunk of cash. Jedd insisted that he be taken care of financially.'

Sitting back in her chair, she took a mouthful of her wine, her eyes twinkling with amusement at Carla's stunned expression. 'So, now you know. And here's an extra little titbit for you... The St Orvel centre's not Jedd's only project. He's got plans to set up another Starship by the middle of next year. When I said he was a very special guy, I wasn't joking.'

'No, you definitely weren't.'

Carla's brain was spinning. This was the man she'd

fallen in love with. She'd never felt so filled with admiration in her life.

Nor so utterly consumed with horror at what she'd done.

Annie was still watching her. She leaned towards her with a scowl. 'So, stop pretending you don't care about him. I know that you do. And I've seen the way he looks at you. He cares about you, too.'

'Not any more.'

Carla felt her heart grow still as she relived those last few moments with him in her room that afternoon. The closed look on his face. His final words: 'I'll see you around.'

'Oh, Annie, I think I've blown it. What on earth am I going to do?'

Carla was on the first ferry to Pentorra the following morning.

'Go to him,' Annie had told her last night when she'd finished recounting what had happened. 'Talk to him. Explain why you did it.'

In fact, Carla had already decided that was what she'd do. And, surely, once he knew what she'd believed about him and Annie, he'd understand and forgive her and this whole mess would be resolved? The situation wasn't really so tragic, after all.

She'd thought about phoning first, but it would be nicer to surprise him. As she strode up the winding road in the early morning sunshine, she was burning with anticipation, desperate to see him again. And she kept smiling to herself as she imagined his expression when she finally revealed all the nonsense that had been in her head.

'Carla!'

She swung round, recognising Larry's voice. And, sure enough, there he was in his old pick-up truck.

'Hi, there!' She grinned, hurrying over to greet him.

He leaned out of the open window. 'Jump in. I'll give you a lift.' Then a thought seemed to strike him. 'You're not looking for Jedd, by any chance?'

As she nodded, he shook his head. 'You've had a wasted journey, I'm afraid. Jedd's gone. I don't know where he is or when he'll be back.'

CHAPTER TWELVE

IT WAS all her stupid fault, of course. No wonder he'd gone away. After the way she'd treated him, who could be surprised that he'd decided to wash his hands of her and disappear for a while? And now what was she going to do? If only she could turn the clock back.

She ought to have known he wasn't the type to cheat on a girlfriend. Especially not like that, with one of her friends. If only she'd tried trusting him, giving him the benefit of the doubt. If only, if only... She was driving herself crazy. And it was utterly pointless. It didn't solve a thing.

'How long do you think he'll be gone?' she asked Annie when she got back. 'I mean, does he ever stay away for long periods of time?'

'Hardly ever; he's totally dedicated to the estate. You'll see. He'll be back in a couple of days.'

But then another thought struck Carla. 'He wouldn't have decided to take a holiday?' If he had, he could be gone for a couple of weeks.

'I don't think so.' Annie paused. 'He is due a holiday, mind, and he was talking of maybe taking a break in France.' As Carla blanched, she reached out and gave her arm a kindly squeeze. 'But he wouldn't go without telling anyone. Especially not with Jasper ill. So, for heaven's sake, stop worrying and just try to relax.'

But that was easier said than done. What if Annie was wrong? Jedd loved his uncle, but Jasper was much better now and, these days, it was easy to stay in touch by phone or fax.

Terror filled her. She only had a couple of weeks left. What if, by the time he returned, she was gone? That would be it. She'd never see him again. At the thought she felt the blood turn to ice in her veins.

And then, on the fourth day, it seemed her worst fears were confirmed. A postcard for Annie arrived in the morning post.

From Jedd. Postmarked Boulogne, in France.

Carla had already decided to visit Jasper that afternoon, though she was feeling so low after the arrival of the postcard that she nearly changed her mind and just shut herself up in her room instead.

Don't be such a misery. Everything's not lost yet, she told herself. Maybe he just popped over to France on a day trip. For the postcard had provided no information whatsoever. 'Great weather, great food, great wine,' was all it had said.

Half an hour with Jasper definitely helped to cheer her up. He was looking really well now and was clearly feeling good too. But even he was no help when it came to figuring out Jedd's plans.

'He's phoned me every day since he went away,' he told Carla. 'But you know Jedd... He doesn't talk much about himself. He just asks me how I am, who's been to see me and things like that. I haven't a clue why he's gone to France, but he keeps telling me he'll be back soon.'

But what did 'soon' mean? In a day or two? Next week? Carla kissed the old man goodbye and stepped out into the corridor, trying very hard to curb her silly fantasy that Jedd would suddenly appear from out of some doorway, materialise like a genie at the foot of the staircase or surprise her by emerging from the drawing room as she walked past.

It wasn't about to happen, just as on the way over he'd totally failed to turn up on the quay or to come driving through the castle gates just as she was walking in. He'd always had this habit of appearing out of the blue—a habit that, at times, had almost driven her mad—but now, when she wanted more than anything for him to show up, he was hundreds of miles away on the other side of the English Channel.

Every time she thought that she felt a shiver across her skin and a tightness like a band of steel round her heart. So this was what love felt like. This pain, this fear, this hope. One minute soaring to the clouds in a burst of wild elation, the next driven to the ground in a storm of crushing panic. But she was in there up to her neck. There was no way out now.

She sighed resignedly as she strode down the road to catch the ferry. Think of something else, she instructed herself firmly. About the kids, for example, and what you're going to be doing with them when you get back.

It worked. By the time she'd reached the foot of the hill and was heading past the row of whitewashed houses that lined the quayside, Carla's thoughts had turned to recipes for treacle toffee—for she'd promised the children she'd make them some tonight.

The ferry was waiting. Carla flicked it a distracted glance. She definitely must remember to buy some condensed milk. Just the other day, they'd finished the last tin.

She stepped onto the quay, eyes focused on the

ground, her brain still busily ticking off ingredients. Butter, sugar... There was plenty of both of those. Milk. No problem. And there were two big jars of treacle.

Carla had almost reached the jetty now. I'll use that heavy-bottomed pan, the one Annie keeps in the cupboard under the sink, and I'm sure I saw a sugar thermometer somewhere, she told herself. As for trays, there are a couple that would be absolutely perfect— She broke off, suddenly aware of a pair of eyes on her.

Frowning, she glanced up.

And instantly stopped dead.

Jedd was standing watching her, less than four metres away.

Carla blinked. Was it really him or was her brain playing tricks? But then, as she stood staring at him, he started to come towards her.

He smiled. 'I'm sorry if I've given you another fright. You've got that look again—as though you've just seen a ghost.'

Not a ghost. Just the most wonderful sight in all the world. An overpowering rush of helpless love and joy poured through her, but all she could think of to say was, 'I thought you were in France. Your card to Annie arrived this morning.'

'I know. She told me when I stopped by the centre to hand in some literature I picked up while I was over there.'

'Ah.' Disappointment tweaked at her heart. For a moment, she'd dared to hope he might have gone to the centre to look for her.

'I've been finding out about pony-trekking holidays for kids. It's something I'd like to incorporate in our programme next year.' He smiled. 'I understand Annie's already spilled the beans...so there's really not much point in keeping it a secret.'

'No.'

Carla did her best to smile back. This wasn't how she'd imagined it. In her fantasies over the past few days, as soon as she saw him she'd run to him and hug him, laughing and weeping as he pulled her into his arms, explaining about the mistake she'd made as he held her close and kissed her.

But, instead, she was standing there as though she were made of wood and he was being so strangely distant and formal. If only he'd reach out and touch her, like he always did.

She said, 'And was your trip a success?'

'In one respect, yes. I got the information I was after. I reckon we'll be able to set up something for next Easter.'

'Excellent. That sounds good.'

'But, in another respect, no.' He paused for a moment, dark eyes scanning her face. Then he frowned. 'I failed totally in my efforts to forget you.'

What? Had she heard right? She felt her heart do a back-flip. She stared at him, at a total loss as to what to say.

He peered at her. 'Is it true what Annie's been telling me...that you were under the impression that she and I were involved?' As he said it, he reached out and, very softly, touched her cheek.

Carla nodded. Now her stomach was doing back-flips too.

Jedd paused again. 'And was that why you told me to get lost?'

'Yes.' She looked up at him, scarcely able to breathe.

He said nothing for a moment, just gazed into her eyes. Then, with a sigh, he took hold of her and drew her into his arms. 'Thank heavens!' he murmured as, at last, he bent to kiss her.

The world had stopped turning. Carla melted against him, her lips burning at the touch of him, the tears pricking at her eyes. And she could hear his words echoing like a song deep in her heart. Over and over. 'Thank heavens!' 'Thank heavens!'

They stood there for a long time. Carla would happily have stayed for ever. But suddenly, over his shoulder, something off in the distance caught her eye. Frowning, she blinked and forced herself to focus.

'Oh, no! What have I done?' With a gasp of horror, she drew away. The ferry, whose existence she'd entirely forgotten, had already left the jetty and was heading out to sea.

'What is it?' Jedd turned to follow her gaze. Then he smiled. 'Don't worry. It doesn't matter. Let it go.'

'But I can't! I have to get back! Annie's expecting me. You'll have to lend me one of the launches!'

'Not a chance. You're staying here.' As she started to protest, he laid a silencing finger against her lips. 'For one thing, I have strict instructions from Annie that you're not to set foot in the centre until tomorrow morning. And, for another, you and I have quite a few things to discuss.'

'But—'

'But nothing. You're coming with me.' He took her by the hand. 'I know a nice little spot where we can be by ourselves without any danger of interruptions.'

'But, Jedd, I—'

'Oh, and one other thing. Annie said to tell you that

she'll take charge of the treacle toffee.' He paused and smiled down at her. 'Now will you come?'

Carla laughed. 'Okay. But where are you taking me?'

'That's a secret. But don't worry, you'll recognise it when we get there.'

And, with that, he began to lead her back towards the road.

Carla knew, as soon as they arrived at the marina, where he was taking her.

She pulled a face as he helped her climb into the boat. 'Are you sure this is a good idea? I mean, we don't want to invite disaster. What happens if we get swept away or both end up with twisted ankles?'

Jedd kissed her. 'I promise there won't be any twisted ankles.' He gazed into her eyes. 'Though I'm not so sure about the rest. I seem to recall we have some unfinished business left over from last time.'

'Oh, really?' Kissing him back, she ran her fingers through his hair. 'I wonder what kind of unfinished business you might be referring to?'

'I think you know.' He laid his hand against her breast, causing a flare of naked desire to twist through her. 'But, before we get on to that, there's something I have to do first.' Before she could ask what that was, he silenced her with another kiss. 'Don't be so curious. You'll find out soon enough.'

They were less than ten minutes away from Gull Point when he stopped the boat.

Carla peered at him. 'What's happening? Have we run out of gas?'

'No.' Jedd shook his head. Then he just sat looking at her for a minute. 'Before we go any further, there's a question I want to ask you.' He leaned forward and took her hand, his eyes burning into hers. 'You'll probably think I'm crazy, but that's just the way I am. I can't go on without knowing… Carla, will you marry me?'

'Marry?' Carla blinked. He was forever surprising her, but he'd definitely surpassed himself this time!

'Will you? I really don't think I could live without you.'

Carla looked at him, suddenly thrown back to that moment in her bedroom when she'd been certain that he'd just walked out of her life for good. She'd thought something similar then. That she didn't want to live without him. And the only thing that had altered was that it was even more true now.

She leaned forward and kissed him. 'Nor I without you.' With a small smile, she nodded. 'Yes, Jedd, I'll marry you.'

For the rest of the short journey, they didn't speak at all. There was no need for words. Their eyes said it all. But as they were wading ashore, having tied up the boat, Jedd suddenly caught hold of her and swivelled her round to face him.

'There's something I ought to tell you. I don't believe in long engagements.'

Carla smiled. It wasn't a subject she'd ever seriously thought about, but now that he'd brought it up she found that she had an opinion too.

She shook her head. 'Neither do I.'

He drew her against him. 'I vote for some time in September.' He kissed her and began to unbutton her wet blouse. 'The beginning of September. How does that sound?'

That was only a matter of weeks away. Carla gazed

into his face as she pulled his shirt free from the waist-band of his trousers. 'I think I'd have to say that sounds absolutely fine.'

'Good.' With a smile, he swept her up into his arms, carried her the rest of the way and laid her down on the wet sand. He stretched out beside her and began to peel off her blouse. 'And there's another thing,' he added as he tossed it aside.

'Oh, yes?' Carla was pulling his shirt over his head. She threw it beside her blouse and ran her fingers through his ruffled hair. 'And what would that be?' she wanted to know.

He was undoing the zip of her skirt, easing it down over her hips. 'We're agreed, I seem to remember, that we both want a big family.' As he paused and held her eyes, her skirt went to join the pile. And then he was doing the same with her bra. 'My opinion is that we should start as soon as we're married.'

Carla smiled at him. 'Funny. That's how I feel too.'

He bent to kiss her naked breasts. 'Two or three. Or maybe four. What do you say? How about a couple of each?'

Carla laughed, kissed his wet hair, and pulled him down on top of her. 'I just know I'm going to be so happy married to you.'

Jedd kissed her again as the waves lapped round their feet in a scene that was rapidly turning into another re-make of *From Here to Eternity*.

'Yes, you are,' he assured her. 'You'd better believe it.'

Jedd stood at the open window and looked down onto the terrace at the most beautiful scene his heart could ever have contrived. There was no doubt about it. He was the luckiest man alive.

She was sitting in the April sunshine sharing a pot of afternoon tea with Jasper, while Freddie and Buster played together down in the garden. He smiled. If there really was a heaven, this was it.

It was a miracle the way everything had fallen into place. The wedding, Jasper's total recovery and the adoption of Freddie, who was a changed child these days. Happy, relaxed and, of course, dearly loved, he hadn't had a nightmare for over four months now.

There'd also been an unexpected couple of lucky bonuses that were destined to make everyone's life easier. Nicholas wouldn't be coming back and Henrietta had gone too. Just before Christmas, she'd decided to join her brother, who was now settled in Brazil, having surprised everyone a month earlier by announcing his marriage to a Rio de Janeiro heiress. Jedd smiled to himself. Good luck to them all.

Carla still hadn't seen him. He continued to watch her, reflecting that not a single day ever went by when he didn't stop to put up a heartfelt prayer of thanks for that moment when he'd finally faced his true feelings. She was far more to him than just a dangerous obsession. He loved her.

It had happened on the ferry back to Pentorra after that impulsive, highly emotional flight to France. He'd been sitting watching his beloved island get closer and closer and had suddenly realised, with a stab of real anguish, that more than anything in the world he wanted her to be a part of it. And to be a part of him. The most important part of all.

He'd waited for her down by the jetty, praying that

what Annie had said was true. That maybe she cared for him a little, after all. Then suddenly she'd appeared and he'd almost died of fear. He smiled now, remembering. She'd saved him that day.

At that moment, just as he'd known she would, she glanced up at the window. These days, there was a very special telepathy between them. It was a long time since he'd managed to take her by surprise.

'Come and join us!' she called. As she did so, quite unconsciously, she laid one hand protectively over her swollen stomach—for the latest addition to the family was due to be born in a few months' time.

He felt his heart lift with love. 'Okay. I'm on my way.'

Then, after pausing to enjoy her for one moment more, he turned away with a smile and hurried downstairs.

MILLS & BOON®

Next Month's Romances

♡

Each month you can choose from a wide variety of romance novels from Mills & Boon. Below are the new titles to look out for next month from the Presents™ and Enchanted™ series.

Presents™

Enchanted™

H1 9802

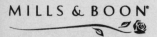

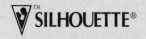

SPECIAL OFFER £5 OFF

FLYING FLOWERS

Beautiful fresh flowers, sent by 1st class post to any UK and Eire address.

We have teamed up with Flying Flowers, the UK's premier 'flowers by post' company, to offer you £5 off a choice of their two most popular bouquets the 18 mix (CAS) of 10 multihead and 8 luxury bloom Carnations and the 25 mix (CFG) of 15 luxury bloom Carnations, 10 Freesias and Gypsophila.
All bouquets contain fresh flowers 'in bud', added greenery, bouquet wrap, flower food, care instructions, and personal message card. They are boxed, gift wrapped and sent by 1st class post.
To redeem £5 off a Flying Flowers bouquet, simply complete the application form below and send it with your cheque or postal order to; **HMB Flying Flowers Offer, The Jersey Flower Centre, Jersey JE1 5FF.**

ORDER FORM (Block capitals please) Valid for delivery anytime until 30th November 1998 MAB/0198/A

Title ....Initials ....Surname ....

Address...

....

....Postcode ....

Signature...Are you a Reader Service Subscriber **YES/NO**

Bouquet(s)**18 CAS** (Usual Price £14.99) **£9.99** ☐   **25 CFG** (Usual Price £19.99) **£14.99** ☐

I enclose a cheque/postal order payable to Flying Flowers for £...............................or payment by

VISA/MASTERCARD ☐☐☐☐☐☐☐☐☐☐☐☐☐☐☐☐ Expiry Date.........../.........../...........

PLEASE SEND MY BOUQUET TO ARRIVE BY........./.........../.........

TO Title ....Initials ....Surname ....

Address...

....

....Postcode ....

Message (Max 10 Words) ....

Please allow a minimum of four working days between receipt of order and 'required by date' for delivery.

You may be mailed with offers from other reputable companies as a result of this application.
Please tick box if you would prefer not to receive such offers. ☐

Terms and Conditions Although dispatched by 1st class post to arrive by the required date the exact day of delivery cannot be guaranteed. Valid for delivery anytime until 30th November 1998. Maximum of 5 redemptions per household, photocopies of the voucher will be accepted.